KASEENO & ROYALE

Lovin' A Vegas Hustla

K. BRIJ'ON

Kaseeno & Royale

Copyright 2019 by K. Brijon
Published by Mz. Lady P Presents
All rights reserved
This book is a work of fiction. Names, characters, places, and incidents either are the product of the author's imagination or are used fictitiously and are not to be construed as real. Any resemblance to actual persons, living or dead, business establishments, events, or locales or, is entirely coincidental.

Acknowledgments

First and foremost, I would like to thank God, who is the head of my life. To all my family and friends who have supported my dreams of being a published author, words could never express how grateful I am for all of your continued love. To the readers who have anticipated this project, I'm sorry for the wait. I thank you all so very much for your patience and for just taking the time out of your schedules to even read the words that I write.

I want to give a very special thanks to Grandma Jimmie "Dollie" Gordon. Thank you so much for being there for me during one of the most difficult times of my life. When I felt like giving up on everything, it was your kind words that helped me push through. I love you and your family so very much.

To Mz. Lady P and my extended family at Mz. Lady P Presents, you gals are the best! Thank you for believing in me and always rooting for me to win. This makes book #3 for me! I hope you all enjoy it.

1

Royale' Lee

"All day, 24/7
Yeah, all day, 24/7"

THE SWEET SOUNDS of Meek Mill and Ella Mai filled the Blue Martini. I stood behind the bar sippin' my coffee watching as all the lovers in the house drunkenly serenaded one another. Any other night I'd be as loose as Grey Goose right along with them, but I've got two nail clients in the morning, and I can't miss out on no money. So tonight, I'm sticking to what's left of my Starbucks' iced coffee. My name is Royale' Lee. I'm a nail tech by day and a bartender at night. Between cocktails and fill-ins, it seems I never get a good night's rest, but I imagine I'll have plenty of time to sleep when I die. Besides that, I'm often so haunted by the shit in my dreams that I would rather be up chasing a dollar anyway. Hell, the paper never rests, so neither do I.

"Two Hennies, one with a splash of cranberry, and can

you have the bottle girls bring two black bottles and the cake over to my section now, please?"

"Coming right up." I sat down my caffeinated drink and proceeded to fill my customer's request.

The man handed me five blue-faced hundred-dollar bills. The diamonds on his neck and wrist danced along with the partygoers surrounding him. I tried not to be blinded or impressed. A lot of athletes, celebrities, and paid niggas passed through here all the time. Still, these stones looked so brilliant and beautiful from where I was standing. The clarity in his jewels was almost like something I had never seen before.

By the time that I had returned with his drink, he was dancing with a beautiful brown-skinned chick. His hands palmed her firm, round ass. I sat the drinks down and tried to hand him his change. He shook his head and mouthed, "Keep it," before winking at me and smiling. I stuffed the change into my bra and tended to my other customers.

2

Kaseeno Menace

"Lovin' the shit out you, fuckin' the shit out you
    For seven days straight, and now I can't even live without you..."

QUITA LOVINGLY WRAPPED her arms around my neck and began swaying from side to side. I grabbed her big round ass like they were two basketballs, and I was Tristan Thompson working on my handle or something. My bitch is so bad with hers that there was not a blemish on her flawless Hershey chocolate-colored skin. On an average day, she looks good, but the way this new honey brown lace closure wig matched her skin tone tonight was just right. Her perfect apple-shaped breasts sat so pretty and perkily on her chest, leading down to her small waist that supports that immaculate ass that I love so much. Her dress was sheer with diamond encrusts tailored made by designer Angel Brinks. It barely covered what her momma gave her. Without a doubt, everyone in the building knew tonight belonged to her.

We've been rocking for almost five years now and she even got my signature dice tattoo on her arm with the nickname I gave her, LUCKI. I call her that cause the day I met her, a nigga swore that I must've hit the jackpot. Indeed, I had. After years of taking care of my momma through her battle with cancer, I finally lost her and was just a broken shell of the man I once had been.

Not only had I lost the woman that meant the world to me, but there is also no shame in admitting that I had lost myself as well, and at the time, I only found solace in a nasty gambling addiction that I had developed. As a result, many of my investments and business ventures were failing miserably. Then one night, I was sitting in the casino down to my very last, and across from me at the blackjack table was Quita. She was the epitome of beauty. If there is such a thing as love at first sight, then a mere glance in her direction made the shattered pieces of my heart whole and able to beat again. I had to have her, and not to sound cocky, but I've been so blessed in my life that there are few things in the world that God has shown me he doesn't allow me to gain.

I finished my glass of Henny on the rocks, lit a fat Cuban cigar, and stepped to her. Not even bothering to ask if the seat was taken, I planted my ass in the chair and proceeded to introduce myself. Once she smiled, I knew she was mine. That night Quita accompanied me back to my suite, and without judgment, we fucked all over that motherfucker.

I guess the rest is what you call history. We've been inseparable. During the first two years of our relationship, I was constantly up, winning not only in terms of gambling and business, but I'd won my joy and happiness back. I had never met someone so fun and kind-hearted. She was the freshest breath of air in my time of despair, and her energy brought my spirit back to life again. Every night she put that pussy right on me until a nigga would fall dead asleep in it. Then every morning, she'd greet me in the kitchen looking sexy as fuck, not a hair on her head would be out of place. Plus, she could slay a meal. Every morning I awoke to a full breakfast spread prepared for a king. She would say a prayer, we'd eat, and after that, I'd leave home feeling like I could conquer not only the day but the world as well.

Looking back now, it's almost hard to image a nigga like myself was even that mentally, emotionally, and financially fucked up. I have to give shorty credit because, without a doubt, it was her love that nursed me back to life. Even though a nigga's always been well off, back then, a lot of the money was tied up in different ventures, and the shit wasn't rolling in as fast as I thought it should have been. It's like she added value to my life out of nowhere in so many different ways. It's crazy how much things change.

I guess the dopamine has worn off, and the honeymoon phase is over. These days Quita barely ever turned the eye of the stove on, which means a nigga spends a big bag on fast food. Besides that, it seems like she only takes her bonnet off when she on her way to the mall. The damn girl has been spending my money faster than I can make it, and it's causing me to be less than pleased. Nothing turns a man off quicker than a lazy bitch.

After reviewing some numbers with my accountant this morning, I can't lie. I'm kind of pissed off, and I intend to have a serious talk with her ass later. For now, I promised myself that I would put all that bullshit aside and just allow my lady to enjoy her birthday party. Tonight is all about her, and as the gentleman I am, it's imperative that I make sure I grant all her wishes. From the way she was knocking the drinks back and smiling, I could tell she was having the time of her life. She grind on me until the song ended. We locked eyes, and she kissed me ever so passionately.

"I'm really enjoying myself bae, but when do I get my gift?" she whispered, biting gently on my ear lobe while grabbing at my dick through my pants pocket. Worried that she was really after my bankroll, I grabbed her hand and locked her fingers into mine. My girl is a lot younger than I am, and her sex drive is through the roof. To put it frankly, her ass is a super freak. If I didn't stop her, she would take a nigga down right here and right now in plain view of all the patrons in the club.

"When we get some privacy," I whispered back to her. She nodded and seductively motioned for me to follow her back to our private section. "Go ahead, bae. I'm just making sure everything here is running smoothly."

Quita shook her head and leaned up to my ear again. "Look at you, always working." I smiled and nodded.

"You know me, bae—daddy's gotta secure the bag. Now get your sexy ass back over there. I still have a lot in store for you tonight." I released her hand and let her go about her way.

By the time she made it onto the dance floor and was no longer focused on me, I turned my attention back to the thick ass bartender working tonight and winked at her. Keeping it professional, she barely even smiled back in my direction, but I know she saw me. Without any doubt, your boy was looking real drippy tonight, but seeing that she wasn't thirsty like the rest of these hoes had me impressed, to say the least. It was clear to me that baby girl ain't even know she's in the presence of a boss, or should I say her boss. It's true. This is one of my many establishments, one of which I don't get a chance to frequent much.

My business partner Vega and I own several night-life establishments in both the Las Vegas and Reno area. My role is mostly as an investor and silent partner handling a lot of business on the back end, like obtaining permits and liquor licenses. Vega manages more of the day-to-day activities like booking entertainment and hiring the staff needed to keep the place running. I know he probably handpicked shorty, and I'm glad he did cause the way she multitasked behind the packed bar was enough to let me know that she's good for business.

I'd have to give him a call in the morning and make sure she wasn't one of the many chicks he's been smashing and adding to the payroll. Shorty was looking so enticing that if he ain't hitting her, then I definitely planned to. Hell, I would just shoot my shot, but with Quita nearby, I decided not to risk it. I already know she doesn't play when it comes to me. As fine as my baby is, don't let her beauty fool you. Her lil' ratchet ass is not above making a scene around here, and a player doesn't move like that.

The tip I left the bartender was good enough that my presence was felt. For now, I made a mental note to get the info, and I just might have to have a little private conference with her in my office a little later on. For now, I'd just have to focus my attention on the birthday girl.

The DJ had turned the party up a little, so I made my way back over to the roped-off VIP section just in time to see Quita's thick ass friend Tweetie or Tweetie whatever the fuck her name is giving Quita a lap dance, shaking her thick ass all over my lady. I know how the two of them get when that liquor gets to flowing through them. They like to fuck around from time to time when I'm preoccupied, and I don't mind.

Even though the whole threesome, group sex shit ain't really my thing, I get in on their fun sometimes since it pleases my lady. Something told me that tonight would be one of those nights. While everyone was wowed at the sight of the large cake and the sparklers in the distance, that almost illuminated throughout the entire club, I took a moment to discreetly pop my esc-pill and prepare myself for the freakiness that I know was awaiting me.

3

Quita Powell

I have to give it to my man Kaseeno. He never fails to treat me like a queen. No man has ever done for me the things that he has done. Not only is he kind, but he is also as hard-working and generous as they come. They don't make them like him anymore. God blessed the day that this man came into my life.

I worship the very ground that he walks on and highly anticipates the day that I become Mrs. Kaseeno Menace. I never want to imagine what my life would be like without him. It's true that there will never be another man for me. He definitely made my twenty-fifth birthday a night to remember. When bottle service came out with all the sparklers and shit, I thought that would be the icing on tonight's cake.

Just when I thought my man was all out of surprises, the music stopped, and the spotlight shined down on me as R&B singer Jacquees serenaded me with his own rendition of "Happy Birthday". When the night was over, my girl Tweetie accompanied us to the service car that was waiting, and we headed straight to the Bellagio where bae had reserved the penthouse fountain view suite. When the door opened, there must have been one hundred balloons littering the floor in my favorite colors, black and gold. There were two gold balloons shaped like a two and five. The entire décor was luxurious.

The wallpaper and furniture trim were mostly golden. Crystal chandeliers hung from the ceilings, and fine art hung against the brown and tan colored designer wallpaper. With one push of a button, the sheer drapery opened, revealing the most beautiful view of the strip that I had ever seen. We were right across from Planet Hollywood and the Eiffel Tower. The light in the fountain below accentuated its beautiful hues of blue. I could even see the LINQ Ferris wheel is the distance.

Below us, the city lights illuminating the strip was an impeccable sight. Just looking down at it all had me feeling like Brandy when she sang sitting on top of the world. You would think that this is just the treatment that a girl gets on her birthday, but the truth is this is just the tip of the iceberg for me. Believe it or not, the multi-million dollar Menace Estate where we live in Sumerlin is just as extravagant. There are so many perks that come with fucking with a high roller, and it doesn't have to be a special occasion for mine to wine, dine, and treat me fine.

Every day, Kaseeno spoils me and goes out of his way to show his love and affection, so it's only right that for my birthday, he spared no expense. He had an iced-out princess cut diamond necklace sitting beautifully in the box from my favorite jeweler, Avianny. Surrounding it was a bouquet of assorted handpicked pink and red roses. What more could a girl ask for? Here I was in this sexy ass room with my two favorite people in the whole wide world, my man and my voluptuous ass best friend.

Kaseeno lit some candles and turned on some soft

sounds of R&B as Tweetie, and I opened the French doors that led to the bathroom. Inside there was a whirlwind Jacuzzi, a bidet, and a walk-in Steamist shower. There was also a small mini-bar neatly stocked with pints of all kinds of hard liquor. Amongst them were Patrón, Grey Goose, and my personal favorite Hennessey surrounding a tall bottle of champagne. We poured ourselves some glasses and filled the Jacuzzi with bubbles and Epson salt.

The sounds of our giggles echoed off the walls as we continued getting drunk and splashing around. Eventually, Kaseeno came in draped in a Versace robe, holding a glass of Henny in his hand and a blunt so big it resembled a Cuban cigar hanging from his lips. He looked like the young black Hugh Hefner. After we were all cleaned up and dry, Tweetie and I ascended to a different wing of the suite and slipped on our sexy lingerie. We ventured into the bedroom where Kasseno stood at the window, gazing over at the traffic near Caesar's Palace.

I joined him, and he wrapped his arms around my waist. He spun me around, admiring the sexy attire. He lustfully licked his full lips and eyed me the way a Pitbull looks at a slab of meat before he devours it. In that moment, it felt like we were the only ones in the room, the only ones in the world even. I don't know what it is that always makes me feel like putty in his hands. It's like the feeling a girl gets in the presence of her first crush. Every single day I fall deeper and deeper in love.

"Did you enjoy your special day, love?"

"You know I did, daddy. Thank you for everything," I said, standing on my tippy toes so that our lips could meet for a French kiss.

"You're more than welcomed baby. Now, I want you to go over there and lay down. Let your friend give you some birthday licks." I smiled excited and strutted over to the bed in my Giuseppe heels.

The lingerie didn't stand a chance. That shit was practically useless because not even five minutes later, Tweetie and I began peeling the articles of clothing off of one another. Kaseeno just sat back and watched in total awe sippin' slowly and taking drags from his blunt. The smoke and aroma of the dispensary's finest marijuana filled the air as she laid me down on the California King sized bed.

I tasted Tweetie's mocha chocolate Victoria's Secret lip gloss as her tongue flicked with mine, I hungrily sucked on it a bit. Before I knew it, we were both completely nude. I moaned softly as I felt the warmth of her mouth, making wet circles around my erect nipples. I pinched at hers and went to lick on them, but she stopped me dead in my tracks.

"Uh-unt. Tonight, it's all about you, baby."

She pushed me back and slowly peeled off my lace thongs, ripping them in the processed. She then used her tongue to separate my pussy lips. Almost instantly, my pussy juices started to overflow as I moaned softly. When it came to giving head, my best friend is the coldest, and she knows just how I like it. She slid two fingers inside of me and maneuvered them in and out as she deliberately sucked on my clitoris. Kaseeno sat quietly in a chair near the foot of the bed, just stroking his dick as he looked on at us.

"She eating that pussy good, huh? You like that, bae?"

"Ummmm... Fuck yeah, daddy! Oh shit, I love it," I groaned in ecstasy, holding her inches back so she could have clear access to my creaming vagina.

My shit was so fucking juicy, and with her skills, it wasn't long before she was, spanking and rubbing on my wet box vigorously, encouraging me to squirt all in her pretty ass face. I made sure to do just that, and now that I had gotten my first nut out of the way, I smiled euphorically and looking at her face all wet with my juices. Wanting to taste my own love, I motioned with my fingers was her to come to me. I sucked on her tongue and licked all around her mouth until I felt her face was nice and clean.

Catching her breath, she smiled pleased with herself. She is always gratified by pleasuring me, and that's why Tweetie is forever my main bitch.

"Yeah, y'all bitches is nasty, nasty, just how daddy likes it. Now, who's ready for this dick, huh?" Kaseeno asked, walking over to the edge of the bed, where we were still wrapped in each other's embrace.

He still held on to his long, thick, hard black dick, and now the veins in that motherfucker were pulsating. It looked like a Snickers bar and gawd dammit I'm not myself when I'm hungry. I immediately got down on all fours and started licking that shit with no hands, slowly at first then I put the whole thing in my mouth and just started going to work on his shit. I hit him with the two-hand twist that always blew his mind.

I licked from the tip, down the shaft, sucked on both his balls, then lifted them, and licked the meat between his balls and ass. Once his shit was as stiff as it could get, I went back and started bobbing up and down as if I had a chicken neck. I chocked trying to fit the whole damn thing in my mouth, including the balls. His shit is just too damn big.

Kaseeno's eyes rolled in the back of his head as he entered into a state of euphoria. I was bent over, and I could feel Tweetie behind me licking from my ass crack and down to my pussy and back again. It wasn't long before she must have got hungry for some dick too because before I knew it, she was at the edge of the bed with me requesting to be fed his beefcake.

"Yeah, share daddy's dick with your friend, bae," Kaseeno commanded.

Unselfishly, and under daddy's instruction, I fed it to her, and she ate that shit up like it was the last supper. That shit was turning me all the way on. Watching her wet slob drip from his dick made me even wetter than I already was. There was nothing that turned me on more than watching my bitch please my nigga. She gobbled on his dick while I tackled the balls. With our asses in the air, he reached down and spanked us both. I looked up at him, and with a wet face, I smiled with lust in my eyes. Tweetie was still deep throating him. He grabbed my chin and kissed me in my mouth.

"You're so fucking nasty. Fuck!" Kaseeno exclaimed, slapping her thick ass again. He looked down at me. "You ready for this daddy dick?"

"Hell yeah," I nodded.

"Turn around," he demanded, pulling his dick from Tweetie's jaws of life.

I did just as he said, and when she laid back, I buried my face in her sweet pussy, while he slowly rodded me out from the back. My tongue slithered in and out of her sweet pussy while daddy put that pipe on me. Her twat tasted good, and his dick felt even better. The best of both fucking worlds left me feeling like such a lucky girl. After taking a pounding on my pussy, we switched positions, and I rubbed on my clit at the sight of his pole going in and out of Tweetie's pussy with slow strokes from the back.

The sight of him fucking the shit out of her made me finger and rub on my pussy so hard that I came and squirted again, and that just drove him crazy.

He pulled his dick out of Tweetie, and I got down on

my knees to catch that nut. Poor Tweetie got down there with me thirsty for some of it too, but her thirst couldn't match my hunger. She opened her mouth, but it was too late. I had made sure to consume every drop. What I didn't catch in my mouth, landed around my lips. Not one to be selfish, I spit it in her mouth and watched as she swallowed it.

Our tongues passionately danced as we engaged it the sloppiest kiss. We both loved the taste of his kids swimming in our mouth. I guess she wanted more because she licked around my face cleaning up what was left of his nut. That fuck session was so damn good. Shit! Happy motherfuckin' birthday to me.

4

Royale'

I woke up in a cold sweat, shaking away the dreaded visions in my dreams, images that I've tried to shake for many years, and yet I haven't been able to. I took a sip from the glass of water that sat on my nightstand. Ten full years had passed since that dreadful stormy night that changed my life. Sometimes when I'm sleeping, it's as if I'm right back there, frozen in that moment of despair not knowing what to do.

Glimpses of that night still appear so vividly in my dreams as if it was happening again in real-time. I'll never forget it was an April night back home in Chicago. The sounds of the thunder outside roared with a vengeance as the raindrops slowly dripped down my car windows. The sporadic lightning illuminated the dark city skies. I sat outside of the apartment building in K-Town, where my twin sister lived with her boyfriend, Slique. It was one week after our nineteenth birthday. They had just moved into the fully furnished one bedroom.

I was staying out in Hyde Park to be closer to the cosmetology school I was attending. Remedi had just started working full time for the Illinois Toll Way Customer Service call center, and her nigga Slique was moving major weight in the hood. She was finally able to afford the cherry red 2009 Mercedes Benz that she was dying to have. She was looked so fly in that car, dressed to the tee in the best and latest designer clothes.

Money was no issue. Shorty was up there, in the prime of her life with whatever her heart could desire at her fingertips. Anything Remedi liked, she got, and if she copped something for herself, more than likely, she made sure to cop me one too—everything from cars, jewelry, and clothes down to shoes. You name it, and we had it.

The hood knew the Lee twins for being two fly ass, bad bitches. We were hitting the clubs and hitting blocks every weekend, and when we weren't tearing down the streets of Chicago, we were busy taking road trips with Slique down to Houston, where he copped most of his work. All the bitches out west wanted to be his main girl, so naturally, Remedi was the envy of all the females from K-Town to L-Town and the Holy City.

Remedi was in her glow. On the outside looking in, everyone thought she and Slique were the most picturesque couple. They were the hood's version of relationship goals, even before the internet coined the famous phrase. Of course, no relationship is perfect, and they had their fair share of fights. It would mostly be because of Slique's cheating ways or because his jealousy was getting the best of him whenever other men paid her attention.

Slique was so possessive when it came to Remedi that another nigga couldn't even innocently dance with her in the club without him bugging up and causing a scene. So, a lot of times, she could just withdraw, and eventually, I noticed that Remedi began to isolate herself. Nobody, not even me, knew that behind closed doors, she was silently suffering the brunt of Slique's violent physical abuse.

On this particular night, I called Remedi before I left my evening classes and told her I was on my way. She had told me that she cooked a large pan of lasagna that evening and wanted me to come over so that I could eat and pack some to take home for my lunch the following day.

When I finally made it to the west side of the city, I sat in my car and dialed hit her number multiple times without any answer. Slique wasn't answering his phone either. Remedi had given me a spare key, so I decided just to let myself in. Nothing in the world could have prepared me for the horror that came next. I walked in to find them both lying dead in a pool of their own blood and guts.

Remy had been shot in the chest and abdomen, and Slique's head was half blown off with a single self-inflicted gunshot wound under his chin. Just the sight and stench of blood made me so sick to my stomach that I instantly began to vomit. I ran out, crying and screaming for help. One of her neighbors peeked out his door and called 9-1-1. Glimpses of the crème colored carpeting drenched with thick blood and splattered membrane still appear so vividly in my dreams. One neighbor admitted to the police that she overheard the two arguing earlier in the day, and Remedi was screaming at the top of her lungs about how she was tired of him hitting her and that she was leaving.

She heard the door slam shut, but when she peeked out of the peephole, Slique was the one who had stormed out only to return shortly after. Another neighbor reported he heard two gunshots, which isn't an uncommon occurrence in the neighbor, so he didn't bother to call law enforcement. I always wondered did she suffer. Did she even stand a chance? I wish Slique had just picked up that phone so that I wouldn't have to find Remedi that way.

Those images still haunt my mind while I'm asleep. In the years that followed, I sought counseling and was diagnosed with Post Traumatic Stress Disorder. My doctor prescribed me some pills that are supposed to help me suppress the horrible memories, but I don't take that shit. In my honest opinion, there is no magic pill that could make me ever forget the horrible way that Remedi was selfishly snatched from this earth. Remedi was my sister, my right hand, and my best friend.

She was literally my A1 since day one. She was the right to my wrong, and someone I thought would always be there. After all, that is how things were supposed to be. It's always been just her and me against this cold, cruel world. Growing up, it was no secret that our mother was a drug-addicted prostitute. So from an early age, all we had was each other and our maternal grandmother.

Granny was a God-fearing woman, but she was brutally honest with us when it came to why momma wasn't present in the home with us. She wasn't naïve when it came to the things her only child was in the streets doing, and she used it as a cautionary tale to teach us not to fall into the trap of drugs. Every Sunday and Wednesday, granny dragged us down to the church, and her prayer remained the same for years. She just kept crying out and pleaded with God for momma to turn from her wicked ways on the streets and be loosened from the binds of her addiction.

Sometimes it seemed as if God would hear her and give her the desire that burned deep in her soul. At least temporarily, from time to time, momma would come home and clean up her act. She would attend Narcotics Anonymous meetings and enroll in the methadone program.

Those were our favorite times because we loved the quality time we got to spend with her when she was home. Despite her shortcomings, we still loved her, and she loved and cared for us too.

I remember fondly. She was a really good mother to us and the most beautiful Belizean woman one could ever feast their eyes on. Mom was stacked like a brick house with a face that could easily rival the most elite of Hollywood's stars. Every night after bath time, she would let Remedi and I take turns brushing her long curly hair that draped down her back. She would show us pictures of our father, the legendary pimp King Ring. He was renowned in the city. As one of the founding member of the Cicero Insane Gang, pops was best friends with the legendary Bishop Don Magic Juan.

He got his nickname because he rocked platinum diamond-studded four-finger rings on both hands. I remember how Remy and I would sit Indian style on the bed and listen intently to the story of how they met and fell in love back in the late seventies before he made a name for himself. Mom was his high school sweetheart. Let her tell it, he had tried his hardest to keep her out of the streets and away from the bullshit he was doing in them.

When she told him that she was pregnant, he made an honest woman out of her, and to please our religiously strict grandmother, they rushed down to the courtroom and quickly entered into Holy matrimony. That was before he became a pimp. Yet, when he did begin to profit off of selling women, all of his top customers wanted to date my mother, but he refused to allow any man to even look in her direction or much the less touch her.

Mom's only task was supposed to be recruiting girls and overseeing them from day-to-day. She made sure they were neatly groomed and looked up to par for the johns.

She was also in charge of the money count, and if any of the hoes was even a dollar short, it was her job to either beat their ass and report to him so that he could beat them. Whenever she went to the beauty parlor or had errands to run, he would have the hoes babysit us, and if we cried for any reason, no matter if it was as simple as a dirty diaper, he was on their ass. She said there was no woman in the world that he loved more than his two little girls.

One night mom walked in on him in the bathroom, shooting heroin into the veins in his arms. After seeing the exhilarated feeling that it gave him, she asked could she try it too. He refused to shoot her up, and he forbid her from indulging in any drugs. He explained to her that anyone who attempted smack could never go back. They would be forever married to the needle until they parted by death. He could warn her all he wanted about the harmful effects of the drug, but he couldn't be there to monitor her twenty-fours a day.

It wasn't long before she found his stash and proceeded to get high off the supply. Just as he imagined, it wasn't long before she was a full-blown junkie. Only then was it that he put her on the stroll with the rest of the hoes. By the time he was killed in the early nineties, she was already using, but that shit turned her out in the streets even worse. It was then that we were sent to live with granny.

At Remedi's funeral, mom was so skinny and frail that she almost looked sickly. Her jaws were sunken in, and she was barely recognizable. Since Grandma was long gone, she was my only living relative I had left. I pleaded with her to enter into a rehabilitation center, and after a bit of hesitation, I finally got her to agree to it, but when it was time for us to meet, she never showed up. I was both shocked and devastated.

Even though I was disappointed, I couldn't be mad at

her because if I hadn't learned anything in the years growing up with a mother as a fiend, I learned that often times, they are slaves to the drug. I just had to accept the fact that at this point, she was just too far gone. As unfortunate as it may seem, she's the last living relative I have. Between losing granny, Remedi, and basically momma too, I went to a really dark place. It was too much for my boyfriend to deal with. Although we remained good friends, soon enough, our relationship was another thing I could add to my long list of losses.

Being in the city had become too depressing for me. Desperate for a fresh start, I packed all I could fit into my Chrysler Pacifica and hit the expressway all the way to Sin City, and I ain't looked back since. I usually talk to momma once or twice a month around the time one of her bills are due. Other than that, the only reminders I have of life in Chicago are the dreams that make my nights dreadful. That's why I prefer just to work both day and night.

Speaking of work, it was time for me to get up and clean my house. I had two clients that already booked on Style Seat, and I was anticipating more would book before the afternoon hit. While bartending is what keeps the bills paid, being a nail technician is what I am most passionate about. I don't just lay acrylic and call myself a nail artist. I cater to an elite clientele, to whom I offer a high standard of unique services designed specifically with them in mind. I've taken the time to learn about each of their health needs to decide on methods for proper exfoliation.

I identify the points of distress in their hand structures and gently massage out the kinks. Week after week, they come, sit in my chair, and trust me enough to share the details of their daily lives in a safe space. As I finish up and apply the last coat of polish, I watch for that glorious moment when I see that their day has gotten a little better and a bit brighter. I live for that moment. It makes me believe in the beauty that life still has to offer. My ultimate goal is to open a full-service nail and beauty bar that services all my clients' cosmetic needs. It will be a one-stop glamour shop for nails, hair, and skincare at an affordable price

I've been working both day and night to save up for a space, while also paying down outstanding debt to get my credit in shape. It's not easy balancing all that and my day-to-day expenses, but my passion for my craft keeps me motivated. I know in my heart that if my grandma and my sister could see the woman that I've become, they would be proud.

Pushing my nightmare aside, I got up and straightened my house before my first client arrived.

5

Kaseeno

Last night was mad real. I awoke to the sound of Quita and her friend snoring, and the shit annoyed the fuck out of me. Undeniably, both of their pussies were tight, good, and wet last night. Still, I couldn't wait until her ass woke up so that we could discuss all this lavish spending she been fucking doing. It seems like these days everything Quita does seems to get on my goddamn nerves.

The lazy bitch doesn't want to work or shit. It's one thing to provide for your girl, but as a businessman, it's in my best interest to see more money coming in than going out. It wasn't as if she was making smart investments. She was pissing on money purchasing shoes and handbags and shit for her and Tweetie. These days they have been stuck to each other like glue.

Everything we do, her friend got to tag along too. Quita's even been acting like she can't suck a dick good without this bitch's assistance. Today is the day that things are going to change. She's either gone find an occupation or move the fuck around and make room for a female that's got something going for herself. All that Gucci and

Prada shit is a wrap until she proves to me that she worth the shit.

Hell, money doesn't just grow on trees, and that shit for damn sure don't rain down from the clouds. If it did, she had better know the drought has come for her ass. Don't get me wrong. Ain't no money shortage over here. A nigga ain't hurting by a long shot, but still, I think it's time she learns a lesson on the value of hard work, the same lesson my old man taught me growing up.

Before I became a successful businessman and one of Sin City's top high rollers, everyone assumed that I would follow in his footsteps and become a world-class boxer. Before I could even walk, I was being groomed for the ring. Literally, as soon as I got past the crawling phase and stood on my feet, my daddy would challenge me by pushing me back down. Of course, my lil' stubborn ass would only get back up again. It wasn't until I got angry enough to hit back that he finally allowed me to take my first steps, and it's been on ever since.

I'm the only son of the late great world-class heavyweight champion Kaseem "The Sting" Menace. Unlike most of these clown ass niggas in town, I'm originally from Las Vegas, Nevada. Born and raised here, I'll never leave my hometown. Why should I when they treat me like royalty. Some people would say that my upbringing was unorthodox but as odd as it seems, it taught me perseverance. Even though we had the best of the best, once I made it clear that I didn't want to box or go to college, I was given only three thousand dollars, forced to get a job, and put out the house so that I could fend for myself. If I could go back and do it all over again, I wouldn't change a thing. It's because of my parents' tough love that I became the man that I am today.

To be a Menace means you have to be a go-getter and

absolutely undefeated. The name is synonymous with everything top of the line and nothing mediocre. Because I wasn't allowed the luxury of simply living off of my famous name, I had to learn how to make it out here on my own, and that's a skill I want my girl to be able to possess as well. If she ever plans to wear my last name, then I have to be confident in knowing that she'll be able to hold us down in the event that one day I'm unable to. With all the successful and bad bitches in the world these days, tell me why a debonair nigga like myself should settle for a mediocre bitch that doesn't match my drive and ambition.

I fuck with Quita. That's my boo, but bae was starting to have me fucked up. So, when she woke up, I got right on the business,

"Good morning, baby."

She smiled with that freshly fucked expression of ecstasy written all over her face. Her weave was a bit disheveled as she proceeded to greet me with the smell of dick and pussy still on her breath. Visions of her bent over with my dick in her while she went to work on her friend's pussy last night replayed in my mind.

"See your guest out and prepare yourself for breakfast. We got something we need to discuss."

Quita rolled over, seductively biting down on her lip, and grabbing for my dick. I politely stopped her in her tracks.

"Aye, naw. I'm serious. Just do what I said, and meet me downstairs. For real." I flipped the covers off me and got up from the bed.

"Alright, baby." She realized I wasn't playing and nudged her friend, awakening her.

6

Quita

I had the time of my life last night. So much so that when I awoke this morning, I couldn't help but smile. On the other hand, it seems Kaseeno woke up on the wrong side of the bed. When he told me to see Tweetie out, deep down, I was worried because daddy didn't seem pleased. Though I was beaming on the outside, I was secretly wondering what I had done wrong. Still, in a foggy haze of all the good drugs and alcohol from last night, all I can remember is a damn good time.

However, it seems this morning I've gotten myself in some trouble with my baby even though he knows he needs to cut me some slack. I mean, it is still my birthday. A bitch just turned twenty-five. I'm in the prime of my life. I got everything I could ever ask for or even imagine. I'm a bad bitch with no kids and a banging body. I have a beautiful home, a loving man who gives me all I need and more, and a thick ass best friend who I love and adore that we both can suck and fuck.

If anybody asked me, I'd say I'm living my best fuckin' life, what more can a girl ask for. The way I see it, I'm happy and my man should be too. Nevertheless, it is my job to please him first and foremost, so when he went into the bathroom to shower, I did as I was told and smacked Tweetie on her big round red ass waking her and leaving my hand print on it. She woke up giggling and thought I was trying to get it crackin' early.

As good as her body was looking lying next to me, and as tempted as I was to fuck her with my tongue again, I knew that if Kaseeno came back in the room and she wasn't gone he was gone have some shit to say, and I did not feel like hearing it. I huffed and used my new gold iPhone XR to request her Uber.

By the time I had showered and gotten dressed, I found Kaseeno sitting at the table looking fine as hell like always. His muscular tattooed biceps were all oiled up and bulging in his white 'Nobody Trains Harder' tank from The Money Team collection. He also had on a TMT hat and some Nike shorts.

He had a white handkerchief spread across his lap and silver platters of food surrounded him. Room service had delivered the bed and breakfast package, which came with an array of dishes. There were scrambled eggs, French toast, pancakes, sausage, turkey bacon, mimosas, and a fruit platter all neatly plated. Instead of eating, he was on the phone engaged in conversation that he ended as soon as he noticed I had walked in the room.

"Aiight nigga bet, my lady just walked in. Let me eat my breakfast right quick. I'll catch up with you down at the gym in a minute."

Kaseeno ended the call and grabbed the cloth from his lap. In true gentleman fashion, he stood to honor my entrance and pulled out the chair on the other side of the table. We smooched.

"Thank you, baby. Who are you talking to this early?" I asked as I sat, and he pushed my chair in.

"Oh, that was Veg. He training for his next UFC fight, I'm about to head down there and check him out." We made our plates and started to chow down.

"Oh, okay. That sounds fun or whatever. So, what else is up? I know you mentioned you needed to talk to me."

"Yeah, one second," he dusted off his hands and went and grabbed some documents from his MCM backpack. He came back and handed them to me.

"What's this?" I asked, looking at them.

"Those are all the transactions you made on your Titanium AmEx card for this past month."

I was confused as to why he had printed this out. "Okaaay, what's the problem."

He balled his face up. "You don't see a problem there?"

I shook my head. "Do you?"

"Hell yeah! I do. I see about twenty thousand gawd damn problems. Let's see here..." he said, grabbing the papers from my hands. "Over three thousand dollars on Louis Vuitton, almost one thousand at The Crayon Case, which I don't know who the fuck you buying Crayons for, another sixteen hundred for spa and salon services at Costa del Sur, oh and my favorite four thousand muthafuckin' dollars at Fendi, twelve hundred at Salvatore Ferragamo. Should I go on? I mean, this shit is ridiculous. This combined with your other credit card bill from last month, totaled up to almost thirty thousand dollars. That's just in one month, and the accountant ain't even crunching the numbers. This is most definitely a problem for me. Your spending habits have become very excessive. What do you have to say for yourself?"

I sat my fork down.

"Well, first of all, The Crayon Case is the best makeup,

and if you ask me those are all valid expenses. The way I see it bae is I do all this to look good for you." I reached over and placed my hand on top of his, but he quickly pulled back from me.

"You think this shit is a joke, but I'm dead ass serious. You're sitting here smiling and shit. Do you see a smirk on my face? I can't lie. I'm fuckin' pissed about this shit. THE WAY I SEE IT BAE is there is too much money going out and not nearly enough coming in. I've been too lenient with you, and if I continue to let shit like this slide, then I'll be doing us both a disservice. See, I want you to understand this lifestyle might look easy, but in reality, I work really hard for this shit. It's a dog eat dog world out here ma, and I wouldn't be a good nigga if I don't put my lady in a position to win. If I gave you a fish, I'm feeding you for a day, but if you teach you to fish, then you gone eat for a lifetime. Let's say we don't work out, or God forbid something happens to me. Where would that leave you? We're not married, so technically, you're not entitled to any of this shit. The only two things any of us truly have are time and money. Seeing that time is money, I'm starting to think you got too much time on your hands, and as a result, you're spending too much of *MY* money. So as of today, all those shopping sprees and spa dates for you and Tweetie, that shit is dead. I'm taking all your cards too and putting you on an allowance. You gone work, go to school, and find a career field, do something to earn an income for yourself, and prove that you can be self-sufficient. Otherwise, you gone move around, because anything that ain't an investment is an expense. Now don't get me wrong. I'll be more than willing to invest in anything you want to do to better yourself and get some more money coming into our home, but I already have enough expenses. I don't need to be footing the bill for all this unnecessary ass shit you got going on. Do you understand?"

I nodded my head, but deep down, I was taken aback by how he was talking to me.

"I can't hear you. Do you understand?"

I felt so belittled. "Yes. Kaseeno, I understand."

"Aiight, I'm gone let you know now I'm gone be on you every day, and I want to see you make some kind of progress, or it's a wrap, and I ain't bullshittin'."

I sighed. "Okay! It's not that serious. I heard you the first time."

I rolled my eyes because his ass was really blowing me. I can't believe he was really sitting here giving me an ultimatum like this. After all this time we've been together, money ain't never been an issue. I admit lately I might have been going overboard a bit, but damn, he acting like I'm breaking the bank or we going broke or some shit.

"Are you dumb? Is it that fucking serious? Are you gonna pay this shit? Give me forty thousand dollars right now. "Exactly! My money is very serious, so while you acting like you got an attitude with all these bills, I should be the one with a gawd damn attitude. Word up, but it's whatever as long as you know this shit stops right the fuck now. Now excuse me while I go take care of my business. Check out time is at eleven. If I ain't back by then, I'll send a car for you," Kaseeno got up from the table and headed out the door.

I was fuming. Usually my nigga is so chill and laid back. I've never seen him get so upset, and never in our history has he made me feel so small. I balled up the handkerchief and threw it on top of my plate of food. Suddenly, I had lost my appetite.

7

Royale'

I was tired as a dog after servicing five clients. After choosing a cute to wear, I was soaking in the tub reading *Taking His Heart and His Throne: An Untamed Love Story* by author Jaz Akins on my Amazon Kindle. All I wanted was this bath and a quick nap before I had to head to the Blue Martini for work tonight. While I was soaking, I heard my phone buzzing on the floor next to the tub. I looked at the screen and saw it was my best friend, Priyanka. Leaving the phone on the floor so I wouldn't risk it falling in the tub, I slid the button across the screen and quickly put it on speakerphone.

"Hello."

"What's up, bitch? What are you doing?" she asked.

"In the tub… what's going on?"

"Don't you want to do me a favor and I'll love you forever."

"You already love me, bitch. You fuck with me, and you stuck with me."

"I know, but I'll love you even more if you do my nails for me."

"Oh my god, girl, you just refuse to just book on Style Seat like everybody else, huh?"

"You damn skippy. Everybody else ain't your bestie, but I am so…"

I sighed. "Whatever bitch. When you want them done?"

"Right now, I'm at your door, and I some brought wine. Turn up!"

"You a slick ass bitch, calling asking can I do your nails like I had a choice. Your ass is already at the damn door."

"Cause, I knew you wouldn't tell me no. Now hurry up and let me in."

"Damn. Hold on, here I come."

"Alright, bye."

When it comes to Pri, that's my girl, so there's nothing in this world I wouldn't do for that girl. We met at a Korean nail shop where I was working when I first moved here. She came in for a fill-in, and it's like we clicked instantly. She was so pleased with my skills that she vowed that the Koreans would never touch her hands again, and as long as I have known her, she's been a loyal client. She referred me to all the other teachers at the grammar school, where she works as a kindergarten teacher.

It wasn't long before she went from being my client to my closest friend. While most people move here from other places, she was actually born and raised right here in Sin City. Popular in many circles, she is a socialite and the youngest niece of undefeated boxer Floyd Mayweather. In my first year out here, she gladly showed me around, and on nights when I'm not working, and I can let my hair down and get loose, she is the first person I call to hit the club with. It's a movie anytime the two of us get together.

I hung up and swiftly let the water out of the tub. I threw on my robe and slipped my feet into my comfy slippers and went to let her in. The bitch didn't get two feet in the door before she started talking shit.

"Damn, it took you long enough. Shit, it's chilly as fuck out here tonight, and I left my jacket at home. A bitch almost got nipple-sicles."

"Girl, don't start with me. I told your ass I was in the damn tub, and it's sixty-three degrees out there. In Chicago, that's considered a heatwave. What are you doing on this side of town anyway?"

"I had an emergency," she said, sitting down on the barstool and placing the bottle of wine on the kitchen counter.

"Damn, really… What happened?" I questioned all worried as I grabbed two wine glasses and filled them with crushed ice.

"Shit, I broke my nail. What you think happened?"

I put my hand on my hip and smirked. "Really, bitch… that's your emergency? I can't stand your ass." This was typical Priyanka. I just shook my damn hear and poured wine into both our glasses.

"Hell yeah! You know damn well my fine bougie ass cannot be walking around with no missing nails like I'm one of these bum bitches, especially when my best friend is the coldest nail tech on the west coast."

"Who bitch? Who?" I blushed, trying to be fake humble.

"You bitch… you."

"EEEEOOOOWWW!" we uttered simultaneously, laughing and clinging our glasses in a toast.

"Come on, bitch. Let me get you right together real fast. I still got to get dressed and go to work at the club tonight."

We took a seat at the small nail station I set up in the corner of my dining room. After rubbing our hands down with hand sanitizer, I removed Pri's polish and removed what was left of the broken nail on her right pinky finger. I found a tip that fit and glued it down and sanded it with my fingernail file. I gave her a sharp, fye stiletto shape and proceeded to fill her nails in with a fresh coat of gel and shape them up. I put her under the UV light for five minutes. She chose her polish, I applied it, and I put her back under the light for another five minutes.

"Thank you, friend. I absolutely love them," Pri held her hands out, admiring her nails. "Bitch, you done did it again. These bitches are poppin'!"

"Yasssss bitch, now I'm tired as hell. I ain't sleep so well last night, so I'm gone try to get a few z's in before I go to the club and make that money."

"Is it hip-hop night tonight?"

"Naw that was last night, and them niggas was in there too."

"Damn, I should've gone. It's cool though cause I'm definitely popping out next weekend. The Money team will be in the building for the Gervonta Davis fight. I got two tickets, so clear your schedule too, bitch."

"Aw shit," I sang while doing a little twerk move.

"Yassssss hoe, we gone find you a man that night. Shit, I don't think either one of us knows when was the last time you had them good ole pipes cleaned," she said as she grabbed her purse, and we walked towards the front door. I laughed.

"I can't stand you, bitch. Hurry up and get the fuck out."

"Whatever. Shit, you know I'm right."

"Bye!"

"Alright I love you girl. Get some rest and have a good night at work tonight, and remember, make the money don't let it make you." I rolled my eyes.

"Don't give me those old Ronnie hoe quotes." We enjoyed one more laugh as Pri walked out. "I love you too, girl. Drive safe. I'll call you before I head out later." We hugged.

"Alright, see you boo."

8

Kaseeno

It's crazy when I came to Quita about her spending habits, she had the nerve to cop an attitude with me, but at this point, it doesn't even matter. I said what I said, and I meant every word of the shit. I stand on it. If she doesn't get her shit together, I'm gone let her go and wish her well. I've been more than a good man to her, better than any nigga she's had in the past. Since day one, anything she's ever needed or even thought that she wanted has been at her disposal, but now, it's like she's taking my kindness for weakness, and I can't have that. She had better get something going for herself quickly.

After that conversation, it's only right that I blow off some steam. Besides being a businessman like myself, my nigga Veg is also a professional mixed martial artist and boxer. He asked me to meet him down at The Boxing Club, where he was in training to compete in his next fight as a Middleweight in the Ultimate Fighting Championship. By the time I arrived, he was already getting it in and working up a sweat jumping rope. We dapped it up.

"What up, nigga? Your ass is late. For a minute, I thought Quita wasn't letting your ass out to play."

I chuckled as I begin to stretch.

"Yeah right, boy, I ain't you nigga I wear the pants in my relationship."

"I heard that. How is the ole lady anyway? I heard y'all showed out at the club last night."

"Man, you know I had to do it big for her birthday, but her ass been getting on my damn nerves lately."

"Trouble in paradise, dawg?"

"Yeah, you could say that. I just had to have a talk with her this morning. She's getting a lil' too comfortable. She doesn't want to work or do too much of nothing other than spending all my damn money on her and her friend. I feel like I got two bitches. The shit is getting so out of hand man that even Jeff, the accountant, been calling me with numbers. You wouldn't believe this bitch racked up close to forty stacks last month."

"Oh, hell naw!" he said as we hit the treadmill.

"Hell yeah! Nigga, if I'm lying, I'm flying, and I know you see my feet planted on the ground. You know I took them credit cards quick. She done lost her rabbit ass mind," I said as I picked up speed and started to jog.

"Yeah, she's trippin', dawg."

"Fa sho'! Aye, but fuck all that. I wanted to ask you about one of the lil' bartenders that was working last night. I'm tryin' to see if that's your work."

"Which one?"

"The cute lil' light brown, big curly hair one with full lips. She kind of looks like the singer SZA."

"Aw, you must be talking about Royale' Lee. Yeah, she decent boy, but naw that ain't my piece. What you tryin' get at her?"

"Man, you already know how I do." We laughed.

"Shit, good luck. You know I already tried…"

"I already know you, nigga. Shit, what's to her?"

"Straight as an arrow, she ain't doing no fuckin' around. I get no trouble out of her whatsoever. As far as I heard, she's a good employee. Always on time, does no fraternizing, barely drinks on the job, and she's very professional with the customers and the staff. Shit, you see she ain't even give me the time of day."

"That's cause your game weak as hell, boy. Watch a real player play."

"Whatever nigga." Veg shrugged me off as we stopped the treadmill and head over to the punching bags. We wrapped our hands, and he put on a pair of gloves. I stood behind the bag and held it while he started to punch it. I changed the subject.

"Aye, I know you can pull some strings and get us tickets to the fight next weekend."

"Come on now, nigga. You know I already got that."

"That's my dawg. Man, we in that bitch."

"You already know!" I took my turn punching the bag before we retreated to the sauna. After that, I showered and headed home.

9

Quita

I sat staring at my computer, attempting to fill out these dumb ass applications, but the shit seemed useless. I mean, what was I supposed to put in the experience section? Holding a nigga down for the last four years? The shit was starting to give me a headache. I'd much rather be out somewhere shopping, but Kaseeno was really trippin'. I almost had an anxiety attack when this nigga took all my credit cards away.

Right now, he was out working, and he made it more than clear that when he got home, he was going to be looking for me to have made some progress. Before we met, I had taken some early childhood education classes at the University of Nevada, Las Vegas, and I volunteered at a local daycare. Even though that was over four years ago, it's got to count for something. I put that down on the application, and then I thought about Tweetie. Maybe she could get me in as a debt collector at her job.

Even though I didn't have experience in the field, she has been there for a while, so maybe she could put a good word in for me. How hard could it be to sit on the phone and argue with people to pay their bills? It sure as hell beats arguing with my man about mine. She has been successful at it for years, so I'm sure she would have no problem showing me how it works. I know she makes pretty good money, so I figured I could give it a shot. I texted her and told her to stop by on her way home.

———

IT WAS a little past 5:30 p.m., and I was in the kitchen cooking cabbage, cornbread, and a pot roast. Kaseeno was still out working, so I figured I would whip up something delicious for him to eat for dinner in order to get back in his good graces. My baby is always working so hard. It's only right that I cater to him like the king he is. I was starting to think maybe he is right, and I could do more. We have been in this love thing for so long, and I'm confident that man only has my best interest at heart.

Suddenly, the doorbell rang, breaking me away from my thoughts. The UPS and FedEx men had already delivered all the packages I had ordered. It was the last batch of merchandise from the shopping frenzy that's got my ass in hot water. I wasn't really expecting anyone other than maybe Tweetie. I stood on my tippy toes and peeped out of the glass on our arch top double doors, and just as I suspected, it was her. She was looking casual and sexy in her Fashion Nova distressed jeans that she paired a black leather bike jacket over a gray cami and a black Chanel bag that I had gotten her as a Christmas gift.

"Hey, girl." We hugged and kissed each other on the cheek.

"Hey, boo! Come on in. I was just in the kitchen putting the finishing touches on my dinner for tonight."

"Good cause bitch I'm sho' hungry. You got it smelling so good in here."

"I know right."

We walked back to the kitchen, and I poured us both a glass of Hennessy and cranberry juice. After we ate, I poured us up some more drinks, and we went into my bedroom to catch the new episode of *Love & Hip Hop*. I'm glad I had invited her over. Just having some company took my mind off of the ultimatum that Kaseeno had given me. I figured I would get her nice and tipsy before I brought up the real reason for her being here.

"Man, T, thanks for coming by. You just don't know I been going through so much."

"Aw Qui, you ain't got to thank me, pooh. You know I'm always here for you. Tell me what's wrong?" she asked, pushing my hair behind my ear.

"Girl, things between Kaseeno and me been so tense lately. Ever since the day after my party, he's been on my ass about me spending too much money. He told me I better hurry up and get a job. Girl, he even threatened to leave me, and it's got me stressing because he ain't ever talked like that."

"Damn, that's crazy. You don't think he's serious, do you? I mean, he's probably just talking shit."

"Well, bitch, I don't want to risk losing my nigga. That's why I need you to do me a favor and see if you can get me in at your job."

"Yeah, just fill out the application online and use my name as a reference. I'm pretty cool with the lady in HR, so I got you."

"Thank you so much, friend! Girl, I feel like a weight has been taken off me. Bitch, I've really been stressin'."

"Aww, don't stress, baby. Maybe it's something I can do to make you feel better." Tweetie put her hands up my sundress and started rubbing my inner thigh and then my pussy.

"Um, suddenly, I'm feeling better already," I replied, biting down on my lip seductively.

Our lips met, and what started as a simple smooch quickly turned into nasty, juicy spit swapping. She pulled my thongs down, and I took my sundress off and threw it on the floor. It wasn't long before, piece by piece, her clothes began to disappear in a pile as well. I laid back on the plush pillows and closed my eyes while she separated my pussy with her fingers and went straight to slowly licking on my clitoris. She moaned softly, enjoying the sweet tastes of my nectar.

Her mouth felt so good and so wet, I opened my legs as wide as I could and starting grinding my hips covering her entire face with my juices. She starting spanking my ass and that shit drove me crazy. I could hear the sounds of slurping throughout the room as she took my clit into her mouth and began to suck my soul out. I tugged at my nipples, watching her twerk all that ass. She spit in my pussy and starting fucking me with her tongue.

"Ahhh fuck yeah. Fuck that pussy, yes!! You gone make me fuckin' cum."

"Oh, yes, cum for me. I love this pretty, fat juicy pussy baby?" Tweetie talked nasty as she fingered me.

It wasn't long before my legs started shaking, and I was cumming everywhere. She giggled with her face covered in my love. I smiled back, kissing her and tasting my own glory. I licked around her areolas and starting sucking on her titties like a newborn baby thirsting for milk. She climbed up top and held on to the headboard as she sat on my face and bounced her ass.

"Aye, yes....yes, fuck yes! Uhn... Oh, baby, I wanna feel that wet ass pussy."

She got on top, straddling me in a scissoring position. Just the touch of her slippery dripping vagina against mine felt like ecstasy. My eyes rolled in the back of my head as she grind on me slowly. I smacked her ass repeatedly, and that was her cue to pick up the pace. The sound of our skin slapping together was music to my ears, putting me in a trance. That shit just starting to feel so fucking good to me.

"OOOOHHHH!!! FUCK yeah! Give me that wet pussy, baby!" I was on the verge of cumming again when we were suddenly interrupted. The bedroom door flew open.

"MAN, WHAT THE FUCK???"

Startled, we both jumped up and covered ourselves in between the sheets. Kaseeno had the meanest scowl upon his face. He looked like he was ready to kill something. He threw his MCM bag to the ground and stormed over in our direction. Wanting to explain, I tried to catch my breath, but I was panting heavily from the pleasure of the sex we were just having and the adrenaline of getting caught in the act.

"Oh shit! Baby we... I mean I..."

Kaseeno wasn't hearing shit.

"Bitch, you think I'm fucking playing wit' yo ass! You supposed to be in here doing something productive, but instead, you in here fuckin' on this hoe!"

"Hoe....Who the fuck you calling a hoe, Kaseeno? I ain't no hoe when you fuckin' on me, am I?" Tweetie jumped up with an attitude.

Feeling the tension of things escalating, I stood between them, holding her back. Kaseeno stepped forward and reached over me, pointing in her face.

"Get the fuck on, you nappy-headed ass bitch! You

were a hoe then and just for sayin' some shit like that congratulations, you a super hoe now!"

"Nigga, you got me fucked up!"

"Tweetie just STOP, okay!"

"Bitch, get your lil' broke busted ass out my muthafuckin' house 'fore you get fucked up out here!"

Still, butt ass naked, I got between them and put my hand on Kaseeno's chest, hoping that my gentle touch could diffuse the situation. "Bae, calm down."

He pushed me away. "Calm down? Calm down? Nah, bitch! FUCK THAT!"

"You're overreacting! Tweetie came over so we could talk about her job!" I started getting loud my damn self.

"Yeah right, then y'all just got so wet thinking about payday, and you slipped and fell into her pussy, right? Get the fuck outta here!"

"MAN, FUCK YOU, KASEENO. I'VE BEEN KICKED OUT OF BETTER PLACES!" Tweetie screamed.

"Yeah, right, bitch! It doesn't get no better than this hoe!"

"Bae stop, she's leaving."

"Good and you can gone ahead with her! I'm done with this shit," Kaseeno said.

Tweetie was already putting her clothes on. He picked up my underwear and bra and literally threw them in my face.

"You thought I was playing? Since you wanna be a hoe, running around chasing behind this bitch, go be broke with her, and to show you I ain't no petty nigga, you can take all the shit I bought with you."

He headed to the closet and starting grabbing all my clothes, shoes, and handbags. Taking back-to-back trips from our bedroom's walk-in closet to the front door, he threw all my shit on the front lawn. He was yelling and screaming about how much he doesn't need me and how I'm a lazy bitch and not on shit. He was also talking about how he can have any woman and how the next chick will be lucky to have him. He said he was trying to upgrade me and make me a better woman, but I just wanted to be a thot bitch. This nigga was in rare form. When all of it was said in done, I stood there with all my shit scattered out on the manicured grass.

Words can't even begin to describe the range of emotions that I was feeling, but to sum it up in four words, I FELT LIKE SHIT. How could he just throw me away like I'm trash? This is supposed to be my man, my partner. I love him, and I thought he loved me too. I've given this man the best four years of my life. How could he just easily throw all of that away?

"GOOD LUCK!" He slammed the door right in my face.

10

Kaseeno

"Good luck!"

I hope the door hit her right where the Lord damn sure split her lil thick ass. As much as I'm probably going to miss bussin' her and her lil thotiana friend down, I was really starting not to even care no more. Like the old heads say, the thrill is gone, and I don't give a fuck how long we been together or how much love I have for Quita. I can't love her more than she loves her damn self, and I for damn sure can't want more for her than she wants for herself. I wasn't playing when I told her to go get her a job and invest in herself. Imagine how I feel after a long hard day of work I come home to find her bumping coochies with Tweetie's old ratchet ass.

Then she got the nerve to tell me to calm down as if I'm overreacting. Man, that bitch is tripping. Other than all the fuckin' we were doing, she ain't got much substance to her anyway, so it ain't shit for me to miss. Well, maybe I'd missed her cooking whenever the lazy bitch did get around to it. Tonight must have been my lucky night because right after I put her ass out, I went to the kitchen to find that her ass had just low-key laid a bomb ass meal on a nigga.

I'm talking 'bout the bitch had a tender pot roast going in the slow cooker. That shit was straight fire and seasoned to perfection. It was some cabbage in the pot and I almost felt bad when I saw that she even cooked my momma's cornbread. God bless her soul. I smashed that shit and went to sleep.

IT SEEMED like just as quickly as the workweek had come just like that, it was over, and already it was one of the most anticipated weekends of the year. Tonight, Davis was defending his IBF title against Fonseca. With this being the first night in a long time that I'm stepping out as a single man. I awoke and called up my stylist Misa, and instantly she pulled up with racks of shit I could choose from. I needed something exclusive to wear to the fight tonight.

When it comes to getting fresh, she knows what she knows. She brought me damn near the entire 2019 spring collections from all my favorite designers from Balenciaga to Fendi, Louis Vuitton, and Balmain. After trying on several different pieces, I finally decided on the LV brick printed t-shirt, with some all-black Balmain jeans and a fresh pair of Louis Vuitton Beverly Hills sneakers that matched perfectly with the shirt. I topped the look off by accessorizing with the LV Pyramide belt, and the black LV Orbit sunglasses. My diamond-encrusted Cuban link with the fat KM medallion set my shit off, and I was looking real decent.

I hopped in the cardinal red metallic Mercedes G550 wagon and picked up Veg. As soon as he settled in his seat, he lit a fat ass Backwood with the dispensary's finest cookies rolled in it. We got high as hell on the way to the T-Mobile Arena. By the time we made it, the stadium was wall to wall packed. Anybody who is somebody was definitely in the building.

The baddest of the baddest bitches had popped out in droves for tonight's main event. Every club in the city would be hosting after-parties, and the Blue Martini was no different, but while other clubs were charging top dollar for parties tonight, we chose a marketing strategy that would allow ladies to get in for free until eleven o'clock. With the array of beautiful ladies in the atmosphere, it's a guarantee that I'll have one, two, or maybe even a few to slide through. I scanned the crowd to see if I could spot any familiar faces, and low and behold I saw one.

A nigga had to blink twice so I could know it was real. My eyes beheld the glory of the most angelic face, one that had been embedded in my memory ever since our very first encounter. I still remember that brief moment I was graced with her presence. She was looking good as fuck then, but tonight was way different. She was in this bitch showing out for real.

Her entire ensemble was perfect from head to toe. Her long Brazilian bundles looked so soft, and her makeup was beat flawlessly, complimenting her already beautiful features. She was on some real fly shit in a skintight black leather dress that looked like it was painted on her. Just looking at her put me in the mind of some freaky dominatrix shit. The only thing she was missing was a whip.

My eyes traced the way her thin waist led down to her thick hips and a nice round ass. She was smiling and glowing, looking like she was having a real good time chopping it up with her homegirl. Baby girl had me mesmerized and didn't even know it. Initially, I had only flirted with the idea of getting with her, and since I'm fresh out of my relationship, I was taking some time to enjoy being alone. In this past week, there haven't been many women who caught my eye, but still, I feel it's no coincidence that here she was again.

"KASEENO! Aye nigga, you stuck?" Veg tapped me, breaking the daze that I was in. I looked up and noticed a waitress standing there with her pen and pad.

"Would you like to place an order, sir?"

"Yeah. Give me a fifth of D'Ussé on ice and send one to the lovely young lady right there in the all black," I told the waitress nodding in shorty's direction.

"Okay. Your order will be up shortly."

"Thank you." I pulled off a few hundred-dollar bills and told her to keep the change.

"Nigga, who you are sending bottles to?"

"Man, to the shorty I had asked you about that work over at our new spot."

"Royale'?"

"Yeah, she's over there."

"Boy, Quita's gone fuck you up."

"Nigga, who? That shit over with."

"Whaaaat?"

"Hell yeah, boy! I thought you knew that shit dead."

"Straight up."

"Straight up and down, my nigga."

I watched as the waitress tapped Royale' on the shoulder and handed her the bottle in the bucket of ice with some cups. She shook her head, and the lady pointed in my direction. When she looked over, and we locked eyes, I couldn't help but smile, and when she smiled back, I knew I had her, and she could damn sure have some of me if she wanted it. Ain't no limit to what we could do. First, I'd have to properly introduce myself.

11

Royale'

The bottle girl came over to where Pri and I were sitting. She handed me a bottle of D'Ussé on ice, and I thought maybe it was a mistake.

"No ma'am, I didn't order this."

"This is compliments of the gentlemen over there."

I looked over to where she was pointing, and there he was once again, dripping in jewels. His diamonds were dancing like a stripper trying to pay her way through law school. Damn! Did his ass always have to look so fucking good? This nigga is fine, fine. He was looking even better than he had at the bar the other night. He was over smiling in my direction, making me blush. It's like I had no control over my own cheekbones the way I was smiling back and shit.

"Who is that?" Priyanka asked.

"I don't know, some nigga, girl. He was up at the bar the other night flirting on the low, but he was all booed up and shit. He did tip me good though."

"Ahhh shit, okay. Well, bitch, whoever he is, he's coming this way."

I looked up, and sure enough, he was walking towards us. He left his friend sitting in their court-side seats and came over to the adjacent side of the ring where we sat. He was fresh as fuck rockin' all black like me. He definitely was in here looking like he had a big bag. As soon as he approached his Tom Ford cologne tickled my nose.

"Good evening, miss lady. I hope you don't mind. I sent this bottle over for your enjoyment tonight."

I could feel the lust in his eyes as they fixated on mine, and I can't deny he had my kitten wanting to purr. He extended his hand. Flustered, it took a minute for me to find the words to say. Pri saw I was kind of stuck, so she interjected and slapped his ass a five. It took everything in me not to laugh at her crazy ass.

"No, sir! She doesn't mind at all. As a matter of fact, she was just about to come over and thank you. Wasn't you Royale'?" She nudged me, and I cleared my throat.

"I was. Thank you, sir."

"You are more than welcomed, Miss Royale'. That's a beautiful name, by the way."

"Well, thank you again, and by the way, what is your name?"

"I'm Kaseeno."

"Nice to meet you, Mr. Kaseeno." He grabbed my hand and kissed it so gently. I could've fallen out in his arms right there, but a bitch had to hold her composure.

"Actually, I believe we already met. The other night when you were bartending at the Blue Martini."

"Yeah, I remember." I nodded.

"My guy and I are having a party up there tonight. You and your friend should come through."

"Actually, we going to her uncle's nightclub?"

"Oh yeah, where that's at?"

"Girl Collection."

"Okay, ma, that sounds decent. I hope you enjoy yourself beautiful. Maybe when y'all done over there, you can slide through after, and I'll treat y'all to a good breakfast or something. Or if you change your mind, give me a call." He pulled out his business card from the Louis wallet that hung from his belt.

"Um, who knows? We'll see." I said, not wanting to promise anything.

"The ball is in your court, baby girl, but if you do decide to slide, I guarantee you a good time, and that's on me, baby."

He almost lit the place up with his bright white million-dollar. He was making this pussy wet as hell. *Whew, down girl!* Thank God that the lights in the arena dimmed just in time as the first fight was set to begin, I blew a sigh of fresh air. I couldn't be sure I could keep this kitty in her cage if I heard one more word from his juicy pink lips.

"Don't worry. She's gone call you tonight cause I'm gone make sure of it," Pri voiced.

I slapped her leg.

"Bitch..." I mumbled under my breath. He laughed.

"I'll be looking forward to it. You ladies enjoy the fight. Talk to you later, baby."

Kaseeno walked away, leaving me cheesing hard from ear to ear. It felt good to flirt a lil' bit. I mean, why not? He a fine ass nigga, and I was most definitely looking good and smelling even better. It's been a minute since a man has expressed some interest in me. Not because I ain't a good catch, but between doing nails and bartending full-time, a bitch ain't been out on the scene in a while.

Prince Charming for damn sure wasn't going to find me at home, but you know what they say God does work in mysterious ways. Las Vegas is a big city. What's the odds that I ran into this man again after serving him at the bar just the other night. Even though I saw him with the other chick as far as I'm concerned, that's not really my business, and I can't lie and say I didn't find him attractive and wouldn't mind seeing what's to him. For now, I just cracked the bottle, and Pri and me went shot for shot and enjoyed the show.

12

Quita

Watching the fight on the small ass TV in the guest room at Tweetie's house, I was balled up under the cover in her bed sad as hell just knowing Kaseeno was there, and I felt like I was supposed to be there with my man. I still couldn't believe how he handled me the other night when he walked in on me and Tweetie fucking. On the one hand, I can see why he got so upset, but still, it's not like I was cheating on him or something, especially since he already knew how Tweetie and I get down. Plus, he doesn't even know that the only reason she was there is because I was doing exactly what he told me to do.

I hate to phantom the idea that we are really over and done, I keep telling myself that we're just most likely on a break now and once he calms down a little, we can talk, and he can come to his senses. Lord knows I miss that man already. We've had our ups and downs in the past, but he's never gone as far as to put me out of the home that we've shared since practically day one. Luckily, I could stay with Tweetie for as long as I need to, and she was even able to work her magic and get me hired at her job. I couldn't wait to tell bae the good news and just make this shit right. If that means that I have to chill out and cut down on my freaky bust down thotiana ways with my bitch and focus more on my own success, then I'm gone do just that.

Niggas like Kaseeno just don't come along every day. Not only is he a smart, successful businessman in his own right, but he also comes from a good family. He's never been married and has no kids or baby momma drama. He's generous, not to mention handsome and built up like a thoroughbred for real. Getting a man like him is rare, and once you got him, he is definitely not the type of man you want to lose.

I laid there watching him go live on Instagram just having the time of his life like he hadn't thought about me in the least bit, and here I was constantly thinking of him. He was looking good enough to fuckin' eat, shining and smiling like he was as happy as can be. Seeing him live his best life without me had me in my feelings even more. How could he be so happy when I was sitting here miserable as fuck without him? I strolled down his page and saw a promotional flier for a fight after party he was hosting at the new venue that he took me to for my birthday.

"Girl, you still laying there?" Tweetie came out of the bathroom wrapped in a white towel, still dripping, fresh from her shower. She laughed as she dropped the towel and began applying lotion to her body.

"I know you all sad or whatever, but baby, you got to get up and let that hurt go. It's plenty more fish in the sea, especially tonight. You can stay there and be lonely if you want to but bitch you on your own cause I'm 'bout to get out here, okkkkuurrrr!" She did her best Cardi B impression.

"I'm 'bout to get dressed now, man," I sat up in the bed and let out a heavy sigh.

"That's what I'm talkin' about, friend. Get up and shake that shit off. It's so many parties going on tonight. Let's fuck the city up, bitch. Where you wanna go?"

"Shit, ladies are free before eleven at the Blue Martini."

She turned around and looked at me sideways. "The Blue Martini? Really bitch?"

"What?"

"Ain't that Kaseeno and Vega's club?"

"Yeah. So, what?"

"So, bitch, I'm not spending my night chasing Kaseeno ass around, and I'm not about to let you either. What you have to understand is that eventually, all niggas come back, but not if you chase them. That shit will make you look desperate, and desperation will make a nigga run in the opposite direction. Trust me."

I rolled my eyes, not hearing anything that Tweetie had to say. Why should I trust her when this bitch doesn't even have a man. Lord knows I love my girl, but everybody knows she's a hoe who can only keep a man for as long as his dick is stiff, and as soon as he nuts, she most likely doesn't see or hear from him until it's time to get freaky again. Plus, the type of men she fucks with are bum ass nickel and dime hustlers that are nowhere near Kaseeno's caliber. Now I'm no fool, and I'm far from desperate, but if I sit back and do as Tweetie does, I'm going to fuck around and have what Tweetie has, which is no man, and that is just not in my plan.

"Girl, I ain't said nothing about Kaseeno. You trippin'. The club is lit, plus it's free, and I'm broke. I'm just trying to have a good time. That's it."

She eyed me suspiciously and proceeded to get dressed. "That's what you say, but I know you bitch. You going to get that nigga back, but it's cool. We can go there and see what's up, but I'm telling you now I'm not with none of y'all bullshit, and if Kaseeno comes with that same energy from the other day, I will not hesitate to mace his ass."

"Bitch, bye! It ain't even like that. We gone have a good time, watch."

"Whatever, bitch! Just hurry up and wash your ass so we can go."

I sprang up, grabbed some towels, and hit the shower. I took my time exfoliating my body and shaving my pussy. Once I was all fresh, cleaned, and groomed, I flat ironed my wig and took my time beating my face. I put on a gray Guess Allison cut-out bandage dress and a pair of Christian Louboutin pumps. I looked myself over in the mirror and was pleased. Of course, I cleaned up nice. I was going to get my man back by any means necessary, periodt sis.

13

Kaseeno

"Nigga, that's what the fuck I'm talking about!"

I pounded on my chest ecstatically when my nigga Tank knocked his opponent out. I put a healthy wager on this game. After Quita went bananas on her shopping spree last month, a nigga had to get the bag back, and this fight just gave me fifty thousand reasons to celebrate. I logged on to my Instagram and posted the promotional flier for tonight's event. I made a special plea to all my lady followers to meet me there before eleven to get in free.

When we got outside the club, of course, we bypassed the line. The whole time I was scanning that bitch hoping that Royale' and her friend had changed their minds about going to Floyd's club. She still hadn't hit my line yet, and it seemed like I was checking my missed calls every couple of minutes. I guess patience really is a virtue, and my momma used to always say good things are worth waiting for. One thing I didn't have to wait long for was for Quita to blow my line up.

She had called a few times back-to-back on the ride over here, and of course, I wasn't trying to talk, so I sent her ass to the voicemail. Damn, it ain't even been a full week since I showed her ass the door. She wasn't even giving a nigga a chance to miss her. Men love the thrill of being the chasers, and by her pursuing me, especially after how I treated her, the shit was pathetic, and she was turning me off. One could only imagine my disdain when I got to our reserved section in the club to find her and Tweetie sitting there sippin' on my good ass Ace of Spades like they belonged there and had paid for that shit.

"Lucki, how the fuck you get in here man?" I snatched that shit from her hand.

"Hey baby, I missed you. I tried calling, but of course, you didn't answer. One of the security guards saw us in line. He recognized me from the other night and asked was I your girl, and I told him, yeah, so he brought us back here."

"Why you lie like that?"

"Like what, Kaseeno?"

"You are not my fuckin' girl. You ain't want to get your shit together, so I told you that shit over with."

"Bae, you're overreacting. I'll always be for you no matter what, and guess what I got a job. Tweetie hooked me up. I start work on Monday. I tried to explain to you that was the only reason she had come by the other day, but it's like you were so angry you already had your mind made up or something, and I just don't understand how you could give up on me so easily like that. I mean, I know you still love me. You just called me Lucki. I haven't heard you call me that in so long and baby, I miss that. I miss us! The "us" we used to be before all this financial shit became an issue. I want to be your Lucki charm again, and I promise to do better if you give me another chance."

She wrapped her arms around my waist and tried to pull my body close to hers. We were so close to one another that I could see the passion and tears welling up in her eyes. There is no doubt that this girl loves me, and at one point, I won't deny that I had a lot of love for her too. She was right that at one point, she was my good luck charm, and we did seem like a perfect match, but this wasn't a decision that I had made overnight. She got way too comfortable in her position as my girl to the point where she quit school, and that was all she aspired to be.

Still, I'm no heartless nigga. I could see the anguish written all over her pretty face, and I could tell this was hard for her. The words that were coming from her mouth right now sounded good.

Towering over her 5'2 frame, I searched her hazel brown eyes and found them filled with worry and questions as to whether we would be together again, but I refused to lie and give her the answer that she was yearning for. I pushed her away as I felt my phone vibrating in my pocket. The caller I.D. displayed an Illinois number.

"Hello," I answered, plugging my ear to hear who it was on the other end.

"Hey, Mr. Kasseno?" Immediately I didn't pick up on the female voice on the other end.

"Yeah, who this?"

"It's Royale', the girl from earlier..." I noticed Quita was ear hustling, so I turned around to talk in private.

"Yeah, ma. What's up? Where y'all at?"

"We outside in the line."

"Aiight, say less shorty. Just head to the front of the line, I'm 'bout to have somebody come and escort y'all to my section."

"Cool, thanks."

"No problem, see you in a minute."

I hung up and focused my attention back to Quita, who was still standing there looking like a sad, lost puppy. I shook my head and sighed. It turns out breaking up with her wasn't going as smoothly as I had anticipated that it would. This shit was supposed to have been over with yesterday, but apparently, for some, letting go is hard to do. So here I was having to break this shit down again, and since my intentions aren't to rub salt in her wounds, I decided that this time, I'll do my best to let her down easy.

"You a good girl, Qui, and beautiful too. I believe in you, but the problem was getting you to believe in yourself. You got what it takes though, to make a nigga happy, but unfortunately, I'm just not that nigga no more. I don't want you to think it was easy for me to just give up on you because it wasn't, but we both deserve to be happy, and I ain't been happy in this relationship for a while now. I wish you the best on your new job and all that, and I see no reason why we couldn't still be friends. If you need a letter of recommendation or if it's any way that I can help, let me know, aiight."

A lone tear fell from Quita's left eye and rolled slowly down her cheek. She shook her head, not wanting to accept that this shit was really over with us. Right now, it looked like she could use a drink, so I handed the glass of champagne back to her. All I could do was give her the real. I couldn't change how she felt about it. In the near distance, I could see our security detail parting through the crowd making a path for Royale' and her friend to come through. I really didn't want a scene, so I opened the ropes.

"Now, please excuse me, but I have to attend to my guest. Y'all enjoy your night, aiight."

14

Royale'

That bottle of D'Ussé had Priyanka and I lit like the lights on the top of the Sears Tower. Something about dark liquor always made me feel like a Catholic schoolgirl, and I just get to confessing shit. Our plan after the fight was to go to Girl's Collection, but when we got in the back of the Uber, all I could do was talk about how bad I wanted to fuck that fine ass nigga Kaseeno. Typically when a nigga gives me his number, if I'm interested, I make his ass sweat for at least three days before I call. However, in this case, I had my drunk ass best friend here to gas me up. If it had not been for the liquid courage, I wouldn't have changed our plans and told the driver to head over to the Blue Martini.

"You gone get you some dick tonight, ain't you, bitch?" We both had one too many drinks, and we were conversing like drunken fools.

I gasped. "I just might." The revelation hit me like a lightbulb going off in the dead of night. Then out of nowhere, almost in unison, we both broke out laughing.

"YASSSSS BITCH!!! Make it nasty. Make it nasty.

Drop, drop it to the floor, make it nasty, hoe." Priyanka laughed out again, but a tinge of nervousness fell upon me.

"OMG, bitch, it ain't funny. I haven't fucked in two years. What if I forgot how to work the dick?"

"TWO YEARRRRSSSS?" she said in her Big Draco voice. "Gawd damn, bitch! I knew it had a long time, but FUCK! How the hell did you manage to go two whole damn calendars without the dick? I know that lil' monkey is drier than the Mojave Desert."

"Don't judge me, hoe. Shiddddd! What am I gone do?" I asked her.

"Don't worry, friend. Riding dick is the same as riding a bike. You may get a lil' rusty if you ain't done it in a while, but as soon as you get back on it, your skills kick back in."

Just as soon as she said that I noticed the car had stopped. I looked up at the big neon lights. We were here, and I could feel the butterflies swimming around in the pit of my stomach. I don't know if it was because it was fight night or because ladies were free, but either way, I never saw so many people in the line. Then again, I'm usually only here when I'm working, so I never have to bother with the lines anyway.

"OMG bitch, look at this shit. By the time we get in, the party is going to be over."

"Hell, naw! Fuck that, come on," I grabbed her hand and drugged her to the front of the line where I saw one of the security guards Big Ace manning the door. He looked surprised to see me.

"Royale', is that you?" Ace squinted as if he wasn't sure.

"Yeah, nigga. You know it's me."

"Damn, baby girl! You clean up nice. What the fuck are you doing here? You ain't on the schedule tonight."

"Shit, nigga, I'm here for the after-party. Are you gone let me in or not?"

"I would baby, but my boss on my ass. I'm sorry, but if you're not working, then you got to wait at the back of the line like everybody else, sweetheart." I smacked my lips mad that I wouldn't be able to bypass the line.

"Damn, Roy. His bitch ass could've let us in."

"Yeah, probably but fuck that. I ain't bout to beg his fat ass."

"You shouldn't have to. Shit, call that nigga. He said he is hosting the party. Maybe he can pull some strings."

"You right. I'm 'bout to call his ass now," I dialed Kaseeno's number, and after the second ring, he answered.

"Hello," I could barely hear him over the sound of the music blaring through the speakers on the inside of the club.

"Hey, Mr. Kasseno?" I said in the most seductive voice that I could muster up.

"Yeah, who this?"

"It's Royale', the girl from earlier." A nigga like him probably had several bitches calling. I couldn't be sure that he would remember little ole me.

"Yeah, ma. What's up? Where y'all at?"

"We're outside in the line."

"Aiight, say less shorty. Just head to the front of the line, I'm 'bout to have somebody come and escort y'all to my section."

"Cool, thanks."

"No problem, see you in a minute."

Once again, I dragged Priyanka's ass to the front of the line.

"My bad, I ain't know that y'all was Kaseeno's guest. Girl, why you ain't say something?"

That energy that Big Ace had before had changed. It

hadn't even crossed my mind to tell him that the host had invited me. Nevertheless, the ropes opened for us with the quickness, and it wasn't long before Big Ace was clearing the crowds so that we could be escorted straight to the back where Kaseeno and his friends were chilling in the VIP section. I was a little taken aback to see him standing face to face with the same chick that I had seen him with at the bar the other night. I was starting to think that maybe I had made a mistake coming here tonight until I saw him open the ropes, and he turned to the security.

"Ace, see these two ladies out of my section, please."

"Come on." Ace put his hands on the small of her back, attempting to escort her. She snatched away from him.

"Don't touch me. I can walk."

She looked sad and salty as Priyanka and I walked through the rope just as she and her lil' friend were being led out of the section. I, on the other hand, wasted no time greeting Kaseeno's sexy ass. The effects of the liquor were still running warm through my system, and just the sight of him ignited a tingling sensation in my vagina.

"Hey, miss lady. I'm so glad you made it," he whispered in my ear, wrapping his big arms around my waist and pulling me into his warm embrace.

I thought that he was literally about to sweep me off of my feet. It was the kind of hug where simply being in his arms felt like the safest place on earth, even if it was for only a half of a minute. I was looking forward to the good time that he had guaranteed us.

"BITCH!!!!"

I was caught off guard by the drink that was thrown at the back of my head. My brand-new extensions were now drenched in champagne. I couldn't believe this bitch really had the nerve to come for me like I won't snatch her ass and drag her all through this motherfuckin' club. By the sound of the gasps echoing throughout the crowd under the music and the looks on everyone's face, they were just as surprised as I was. I lunged full speed at her ass and cracked her in her shit twice before the security guard, and Kaseeno broke it up.

Before I knew it, he had me lifted in the air. I was kicking my feet, trying to break free. All of a sudden, I looked over and saw Pri fighting the girl's friend. She had her dry ass weave wrapped around her knuckles and was giving her ass all face shots with her other fist. It wasn't long before more security swarmed in and broke them apart and dragged those hoes out of the club. Amid the chaos, I noticed that I had lost the clutch purse I had been carrying. Anxious to get out of his grasp, I swung my foot back and kicked him right in his balls. He immediately dropped me, doubling over in pain.

"WHERE'S MY SHIT AT?" I scrambled, looking for my belongings, but I could find it anywhere.

"Fuck that! Come on, girl..." I grabbed my best friend and made sure that she was straight. "...cause I ain't for none of this goofy ass shit. These niggas can't control their hurting ass hoes. Let's go!"

I was pissed and extremely embarrassed. I am a grown woman and a true queen out here. I have too many goals and too much ambition to be out here misrepresenting myself and stooping down to these bitches' level because of their insecurities, especially over a man that I'm not fucking. Hell, I don't even know this nigga, yet here we are. He done guaranteed us a good time, and as soon as we walked in the door, it's some ambush type shit. Kaseeno and his ole thirsty ass bitch got me fucked up. They can keep the bullshit. I grabbed my friend and got the fuck up out of there. As far as I'm concerned, this shit show is over.

15

Quita

This nigga and this raggedy hoe got me fucked up! See, the way I see it, this shit is far from fucking over. After I wore my heart on my fucking sleeve and laid it all on the line to Kaseeno, I couldn't believe that this nigga actually had the audacity to try to stunt on me and put me out of his section. Then he had the nerve to want to be all up in there with some random ass bitch. He got me more than fucked up, and I made sure to show his ass and that slutty hoe.

What I did in the club was nothing but an introduction so that all these lil' new bitches can know not to play with me over mine. I thought I'd be kind and let her have my drink right in her motherfuckin' face when I saw that hoe looking thirsty. Even though Kaseeno is in his feelings right now, talking all kinds of bullshit, as far as I'm concerned, that's still my nigga, and I'm not ever about to allow him to disrespect me with some new bitch that just popped up out nowhere. These bitches haven't put in the grind, time, or work. They surely weren't there for him when shit was intense.

I was beside him in the trenches when he was down bad, going through depression dealing with the loss of his mother. On the nights when he would come home stressing over bad business dealings or lost wagers, I'm the one who rubbed his back and told him that better days would come and indeed they did. These hoes want to be a nigga's main bitch so bad and don't even know what it takes to hold it down. Ain't no way that after all the hard work I did building him back up, that I'm about to allow the next bitch to come in and have any part of him. So, to see him all hugged up with another woman had me more than furious.

I can't stunt, I wasn't expecting this bitch to get a couple of good punches in before security broke us up, but amid the chaos, I scooped up her clutch purse. YUP, SNATCH! Let me get that hoe. I got all her shit—her phone, keys, I.D., debit, and credit cards—her whole fuckin' identity in my hands.

I don't know what I'm going to do about Kaseeno, but I know I'm gone get my lick back on his new lil' mystery bitch. I got a trick for that hoe. Today is my first day in training for my new job, and a bitch got access to all kinds of tools and search engines. Anything I want or need to know about a bitch is right at my fingertips with the click of a button. They done gave access to the wrong one cause I'm 'bout to get on her ass.

While the trainer was talking, I was entering this hoe's social security number into the Accurint system. I wanted to know exactly who this bitch is and to see what her business was with my man. I scanned all the addresses that came up, and most of them were in Chicago. Only one was here in Las Vegas. It was the same one on her I.D. I clicked on the employment verification tab and the damn club was listed as her place of employment.

That shit blew me away! Not only was this nigga out here fuckin' around already, but he also has the nerve to be fuckin' with the help. Now I was wondering if all that time spent working was all really a bullshit excuse for him to be running wild with this hoe. I wanted to know exactly how long has this bullshit been going on. Is this the reason why he's been around here moving funny, not valuing our relationship, and ready to sacrifice the love we've worked so hard to build? My blood began to boil as I got heated all over again.

I could feel my heart swelling as it filled with envy and vengeance. If this nigga thought he was about to just up and dismiss me after all these years and after all that I've invested in our relationship, he was wrong. If he thought that I'm gone allow him to move on with this random hoe, he got another thought coming. Shit won't be that easy for either one of them because I'm definitely gone be a problem. As the old saying goes, *HELL HAS NO FURY LIKE A WOMAN SCORNED!*

16

Kaseeno

I tried my best to be both sincere and sympathetic with Quita but also clear and concise when I broke it down and let her know that what we shared is now over. Sometimes things just don't work out in a relationship, and that's not to place blame on one party or another. Personally, I don't know why two grown people who claimed to have love for one another can't wish one another well and move forward amicably if and when the relationship has run its course. This relationship has most definitely run its course. I don't understand why she would conduct herself the way she had in my establishment the other night knowing gawd damn well I'm not with that causing scenes shit.

All that drama and fighting shit is a turn off for me. She made herself look pathetic, and if there was any chance that I'd still fuck with her, she definitely ruined it with her disgusting behavior. The little stunt she pulled had me pissed. I had been anticipating seeing Royale' again after the fight, and just as soon as she was escorted into my section, this bitch Quita just had to come along and try to fuck shit up. I was surprised to even see her waiting in my section before I even got there.

I don't even know how she knew about the party, especially since I hadn't invited her ass out. Since that night, she has been blowing my phone up, and it was starting to feel like the bitch was stalking a nigga. Meanwhile, I felt so bad that she had ruined the night for Royale' and me. I felt even worse when she kicked me in my ball sack. I tried calling her a few times so that I could at least apologize.

It's my fault that she even got caught in the crossfire of Quita's bullshit, and I want a chance to make things right. Every time I dialed the number, her phone was going straight to the voicemail. I was starting to think maybe she had put me on the block list. With Vega still training for his fight, I was taking over things at the club for a while. I sat behind the desk in my over-head office. Through the one-way glass, I overlooked a circular view of the entire club.

According to the shift schedule, she should have been here an hour ago. Yet, every time I glance over to the bar, she's not there. I tried her number again, this time from the office phone. Still, I was only getting her voicemail. I waited and watched.

As the clock ticked and tocked, and time continued to pass, there was still no sight of her, and I was beginning to worry. According to her employee profile, she had never missed a day, and after what went down here, I feared that maybe this was a sign that she was never coming back. Just the thought that it might be possible I'd never see her again bothered me. The vibration of my phone against the desk shook me from those dreadful notions. I was hoping that it would be her calling, but of course, it was Quita again for the umpteenth time.

The bitch was starting to annoy the fuck out of me. I

pressed the red button and sent her to the voicemail, and she started calling back-to-back and texting so much that I just went ahead and put her ass on the block list. At this point, I only wanted to hear from one woman, and it damn sure ain't Quita. I reclined in my chair, frustrated. I redialed Royale's number. This time it rang out several times before going to voicemail, and finally, I had some sense of relief. At least now I knew that she was alright, and that I wasn't on her block list. Perhaps all this time, her shit was dead.

I left a quick message.

"Hey, miss lady. It's Kaseeno. I have been trying to reach you. Listen, I'm so sorry about the other night, ma. I had no idea my ex was coming through, and I apologize, her behavior was despicable, and I really hope that you will give me a chance to make it up to you. Give me a call back when you get this message, aiight. Call me back."

WHEN I AWOKE the next morning, I checked my notifications and shorty still hadn't texted or called back. All I had was an email from the casino, notifying me that my line of credit had been increased, which is good news seeing that the bulk of my income comes from gambling. I'm a big fish, and the casinos love to see me coming because they know that I'm bringing that bag with me. They accommodate me well with all kinds of perks like access to the private jets, invites to the most exclusive parties and tournaments, all-expense-paid hotels, you name it. Whenever I show up, I bet the whole house.

I fuck the crap tables up every time and end up leaving with double my money. While my business ventures generate a decent income, I hit the tables to check a real bag. Plus, the thrill of the game alone is always so exciting, and on a day like today, I need to blow off some steam, and what better way other than a good ole game of craps?

I hit the high limit table at the Venetian and immediately raised the stakes higher. I won almost fifty thousand before it was time to head to the club and prepare for the opening. When I went in and rechecked the schedule and saw that Royale' was down to work, I immediately called downstairs to my assistant manager's office.

"Blue Martini. How can I help you?" the receptionist answered after the first ring.

"Good evening Jen. One of the bartenders was a no call/ no show last night, and she's been placed on the schedule tonight?"

"Which one?"

"Royale' Lee."

"Yeah, she's scheduled for today, and she's late. Should we put her on the DNR list?"

"What's that?"

"Do Not Return."

"Oh, naw. When she gets in, send her to my office, please."

"Ok."

"Anything else, sir?"

"No, that's it."

"You got it."

"Thank you."

Little did Miss Royale' know, I got a few tricks up my sleeve to get back in her good graces and make her forget all about the lil' fiasco that occurred the other night. I promised her a good time, and I'm determined to still make that happen. Only she wasn't making it easy with constantly ignoring my calls. By now, I had left her the voicemail and sent text messages, all of which have gone ignored. If shorty didn't want to answer my calls or respond to my messages than I guess I would have to pull my rank and make her come to me.

17

Royale'

Ever since that dreadful fight night, things had been hectic for me. I missed work because I had to have a locksmith change the locks at my apartment. Priyanka ran me around town. I had to purchase a new phone and go to the dealership where I had to get new keys cut for my car. We went to the Department of Motor Vehicles and the social security administration to get a new I.D. and social security card.

    I had to call and have all of my credit and debit cards canceled, and now I'm waiting on them to be reissued. The shit was a real hassle and inconvenient as fuck, but finally, I had pretty much gotten all my shit together, and now I was finally ready to return to work. I just hope I don't run into that crazy ass bitch again because, honestly, I don't have time for the bullshit, but don't get it twisted. I'm from Chicago, so I'm definitely with all that fuck shit. She and that nigga could keep that clown ass shit for themselves. Ever since I replaced my phone, he has been tearing my line down, but he will get no response from me period.

Kaseeno & Royale

I have far too much going on to fuck around and get caught up in this man's drama. After doing my client's a pedicure and full-set with bling, I grabbed my things and hightailed it down to the club to start my shift. Even though I was already late, I clocked in and headed to the locker room to change into my uniform. I was startled to hear them calling for me on the intercom.

"Royale' Lee report to the general manager's office."

FUCK! I knew this had to be about my attendance. Last week I was late twice, and yesterday I was absent and couldn't even call because I didn't have my damn phone. That's two points alone, which means that they could terminate me. From what I've seen, Mr. Vega seems pretty cool. I'd just explain everything to him and pray that he would allow me to keep my job. I knocked on the closed door.

"Come in!"

"You wanted to see me?" I said, pushing the door and peeking in, not expecting to see the nigga Kaseeno. I rolled my eyes and smacked my lips. He was unfazed by my attitude.

"You're late, but I'm glad you at least decided to join us today. Please have a seat."

Confused, I chuckled and closed the door behind me. I sat down across for Kaseeno and watched as he signed the last of the checks that were piled in front of him.

"What are you doing here? Don't tell me you're..."

"Kasseno Menace of Menace Holdings LLC, your boss." He extended his hand for me to shake, but I just smirked and rolled my eyes. He smiled at me and without even thinking, I smiled back. The charmed that exuded off of him was undeniable.

"Oh my god, quit playing." He laughed.

"You see, Ms. Lee. I don't play, especially not on the clock. My time is money, and when my employees don't show up or even show up late, that costs me," he said, checking his Audemars Piguet wristwatch.

"So, what I'm fired?"

He flashed that enticing smile again, and it made me so moist I shifted a bit in my seat. I wanted to lay his ass flat on that desk and ride that dick to the "Old Town Road". The sexual tension was definitely in the air as he got up from his chair and walked closer. The Sauvage by Dior cologne he wore tickled my nose as his 6'3 stature towered over me. I hungrily bit down on my bottom lip, fighting the urge to lick his dick print that was now staring me in the eye. He sat down on the edge of the wooden desk in front of me, and I watched his lips intensely waiting for what he would say next.

"Just the opposite. Actually, I'm gone give you a raise and some paid time off under one condition."

I raised an eyebrow. "Yeah? And what's that?"

"You get to spend some of that time with me." Another smile escaped my cheekbones.

"Well, you're just full of surprises, aren't you?"

"There's actually much more where that comes from. Plus, it's the least I could to apologize for what took place the other night. If you would allow me to, I'd love to take you on a real date. This time just the two of us and no interruptions."

I stood up and looked him in his hazel eyes, "Why not? After all, nothing can be worse than the other night. I'm sure. Just let me know when and I'm down."

"No better time than right now, miss lady."

"Right now? Naw, I'm not prepared right now. Look at me."

"You look perfect to me. I mean, I ain't gone let you step out unprepared or whatever but damn a nigga scared you gone slip away again. So how about whatever you need, we'll get on the way there."

"Say less."

18

Quita

"Girl, what the fuck are you doing?" Tweetie crept up behind me, causing me to jump. I clutched my imaginary pearls.

"WHOO! Damn bitch, don't scare me like that."

"You have been sitting at that damn computer for over an hour."

"Shit, I'm building my fake profile so I can keep track of Kaseeno and this Royale' bitch." Tweetie rolled her eyes.

"You still on that? It's a million other niggas in Vegas. You need to let Kaseeno's ass go, bitch. What's it gone take? He already embarrassed your ass when he kicked us out of the club and stayed behind with her. He made it very clear that y'all are over. At this point, your ass trippin'. I could never."

"Yes, bitch! We both know you could NEVER get a man that fine with the kind of bankroll mines got, and if there are so many niggas out here, then why the fuck you can't seem to keep one?"

It was true, as bad as Tweetie is, the bitch might be

able to get a rich nigga to fuck her, but they never wifed her ratchet ass up. It might've been a low blow, but right now, this bitch was pissing me off. She of all people should know that this whole break up with Kaseeno has been a sensitive topic for me. Instead of talking shit, I just need her to be a shoulder to lean on and a face to sit on during this difficult time.

"Whatever, bitch, you the one gone be all alone at your pity party tonight. I'm gone."

I got up just long enough to close the door behind her irritating ass. I wasn't stuttin' that bitch. I was far too busy building my fake Facebook profile. To make it look real, I used some pictures of this lame ass nigga that she used to fuck with. My first order of business was to add enough friends to make the shit look legit, and for good measure, I even added some of lil Miss Royale's friends. Of course, I definitely sent her and Kaseeno friend requests.

I know Kaseeno barely uses social media, so I already knew it might be a while before he responded, but I didn't expect that she would accept the request so fast. I was glad she did though. I went through all her pictures. I came to find out that the bitch was a twin and a nail technician. Most of her pictures were of her work, and there were a few of her and her lil' friend partying in the clubs. I had to admit that this bitch was bad.

I really couldn't find one flaw in her, and that shit made my blood boil. I came across a screenshot of her Snapchat code and figured that I would add her there too so I could see whatever else there was to see, and low and behold this bitch was snapping it up on the beautiful patio at Lakeside, my favorite restaurant at the Wynn. The nerve of this nigga to take her to what was supposed to be our spot. He must really be feeling her because he was definitely pulling out all the stops. The scenic view overlooking the Lake of Dreams is enough to make any bitch give up the panties.

Seeing her gush over the live jazz band and the amazing seafood, knowing that she was enjoying this magical night with the man that I love, I'd be lying if I said the shit didn't hurt, yet and still, I couldn't stop watching. It was like I was obsessed. I wanted to know every detail and every move that the two of them were making. The longer I watched, the more envious I became. If I thought that him taking her to my favorite restaurant was bad, what came next was enough to make a bitch like me want to shed a tear.

19

Kaseeno

"A helicopter ride! Wow, are you for real?"

The look on Royale's face was priceless. Her eyes lit up like a billboard in Times Square. In this moment, she was like a kid again, and I knew that I had her right where I wanted her. Tonight, I have every intention of showing Royale' shit that she's never seen before. I laughed at her amazement as she surveyed the helicopter I was able to book with my homie on short notice.

"I'm dead ass serious, baby. Shit, gone 'head, get in." Royale' smiled and proceeded to kick her lil' heels off. I helped her get up there then climbed in after her.

I don't know what was more beautiful, the view of the city's strip with all its illuminating lights or the gorgeous lady on my arm tonight. Royale's smile was a ray of splendor. I could live in this moment just watching as she gazed down in awe of the sight below. It's something about watching someone experience something grand for the very first time. It was my pleasure to be able to show her something new. Little did she know, if she allows me to, I'll show her something new every day and give her something good every night.

We enjoyed the complimentary champagne and strawberries and circled the strip one last time before jetting off to see the Grand Canyon. I watched her as she silently gazed down out of the window. She had this look on her that I just couldn't read. The aura surrounding her let me know that she was in deep thought, and I wanted to know just what was on her mind. Hell, I want to know everything I could about her. I placed my hand on top of hers and brought her focus back to me.

"What's on your mind?" Royale' looked at me with a tinge of sadness in her eyes.

"You really wanna know?"

"I wouldn't have asked if I didn't."

"My sister," she replied, looking down. I lifted her chin so that she would be looking at me again.

"I don't get it, baby. Why are you looking so down?"

A lone tear fell from Royale's eye, and I wasted no time wiping it away. Damn, this was our first date, and already, she had my heart. One tear turned into two, and before I knew it, there was a puddle on my shoulder. I didn't even ask another question. I just held her until she got it all out, and when she finished, she blew her nose and apologized.

"I'm so sorry. Here we are thousands of feet in the air, and I'm crying. You must think I'm crazy."

"Naw, ma. I just don't understand why the tears and how I can make them disappear."

"That's sweet, but there's nothing that you can do. In fact, there is nothing no one can do." Royale' sighed heavily. "She's gone forever."

"Your sister?" I asked, and she just nodded and rested her head back on my shoulders.

"My twin."

"What happened?"

"I don't know. I mean... I should have been there, but I had no idea. None of us knew that she was in an abusive relationship. It wasn't until one night I walked in and I saw it, and now I can't un-see it. I'll never be able to un-see..." Royale' broke down again. She covered her eyes and fell over into my lap, bawling her eyes out.

"Shhh... I'm sorry, baby. I'm so sorry. Damn, I don't know what to say. Shit, where the nigga at? I can make some calls and get his ass dealt with."

Royale' sniffed back her tears and forced a remnant of a smile.

"Thanks, that sounds good, but the bastard is already dead."

"Damn, somebody beat me to it."

"He committed suicide. After he killed her, 'til this day, the shit haunts me. I can't sleep at night. I don't even know why I try. I pray that she'll visit me in my dreams if only for a moment just to tell me that she made it to heaven. I need her to give me a sign or something, but I get nothing, not one sweet fucking dream, nothing but these horrendous nightmares."

"Damn, I'm so sorry to hear that baby."

"You don't have to apologize."

"I just don't know what else to say but if you leave it to me I'll try my hardest to make those bad dreams go away."

"How?"

"I don't know. I guess I'll just fulfill your good dreams." Royale' chuckled.

"You kidding, right?"

"Not at all. Just try me. What's your wildest dream and watch me make it a reality. Tell me."

"I don't know."

"What you mean, you don't know. Come on. There's got to be something that your beautiful heart desires."

"Well, I have been saving and trying to get my nail spa off the ground."

"That's easy, baby. That's material. Money can buy that. You gotta dig deeper than that."

"Well, you asked what my dream is."

"Let me rephrase it then. If you could choose one thing in this world that you've always wanted, what would it be?"

"My mama to get her shit together, Lord knows since Remy's been gone, I've needed her now more than ever."

Royale' told me the story of her childhood and how fucked up on dope her mom is back in Chicago. With each word that left her lips, more and more, I knew that if I wanted to be her nigga than my job would be to mend that broken heart of hers. For every day in her life that had been filled with rain, I vowed to make the sun shine again.

The helicopter landed, but in the morning, I'd be back in the air. After all, I'd never been to the windy city.

20

Royale'

Knock, Knock. I heard the banging on the door, but I was so sleepy that I didn't wanna answer it. KNOCK, KNOCK. The shit was only getting louder, so I woke up and threw on my robe.
  "GAWD DAMMIT! WHO IS IT?"
  I swung the door open so fast that sucker almost flew off the hinges. However, nothing could have prepared me for what I saw standing on the other side. I had to wipe the cold out of my eye cause I was either tripping or a bitch was really seeing a ghost.
  "Well, are you going to just stand there? Fuck it bitch, move. I'll invite my damn self in," she said, pushing past me.
  I was stunned. I mean truly in awe.
  "Remy?" She was still dressed in the same blood-soaked clothes that she wore the night I found her and Slique sprawled out dead on the floor.
  "Yeah, why are you acting so weird sis, damn. What you got to eat in here?" She opened the fridge and bent down carefully examining all of its contents.
  "What are you... I mean, how did you...." I couldn't even gather my thoughts enough to form a full sentence.

"*Ghee, your ass is tweaking. I don't understand. Let it out, bitch.*"

"*You don't know, do you?*" Tears started to well up in my eyes, but I didn't want to let any fall. She looked so happy, like her real self, and I didn't want to put a damper on that. I was afraid that maybe if she sensed something was wrong, she would be scared away. Still, I couldn't hide what I was really feeling, and before I knew it, the waterworks had begun, and those tears escaped my tear ducts and were falling down my face.

"*Oh, sister, don't cry, baby. It's ok. It really is okay. Come here,*" she pulled me into her warm embrace. "*That's why I'm here to let you know that you need to stop all that.*"

"*All what?*"

"*This depressed ass shit. What you thought I didn't know? I know, Roy. I feel what you feel. Shit, you're part of me. So, dry your pretty little eyes, and don't cry no more, sis.*"

"*But I don't have nobody.*"

"*That's a lie. I'm always here for you, and baby girl, you know I love you until the end of time. So, perk up.*"

I sniffed back my tears. "*Okay.*"

"*Okay? Cool!*" Remy said, wiping the last tear from my cheek. "*I gotta go now.*"

"*NO!*" Just that quick, I grew hysterical again, crying and reaching out for her, but as fast as she had come, just like that, she was gone again.

I woke up in a puddle of my own sweat and tears. This dream was like no other. It was different from the others. For years, everyone has been telling me to move forward and just leave the past in the past, and I didn't understand. How can you leave your sister in the past? I couldn't just move on without knowing that she was okay, and this whole time she's been fine, and I'm the one who wasn't ok. I asked God to allow her to visit me one last time and he did. I needed this dream confirmation from the heavens.

R.I.P. Remedi Shanda Lee
January 10, 1989 - July 16, 2018

21

Quita

It was yet another night sitting at home depressed as fuck. This was becoming my routine every night since Kaseeno left. Speaking of Kaseeno, I wondered what he was doing right now. I was trying my hardest to move on and get over his ass, but who was I kidding? That dick hit different, and I can't fool myself.

Hell, I wanted it, but I already know after that lil' stunt I pulled fighting in his club, Kaseeno was not going to be fucking with me no time soon. Anyone that knows Kaseeno knows that he is very easily embarrassed, and he does not like bitches that make scenes. Still, when the time presented itself, I did what I felt needed to be done because I'm not one to stand for the embarrassment. I'm going to sit around while he out on the town flaunting this bitch as if she's his main lady. It should be me right there on his arm, enjoying the limelight. After all, I was the same bitch that went through the trenches with him. In my heart, I know Tweetie is right when she told me to shake this shit off and forget about him, but it ain't that easy. Every day I miss Kaseeno more, and I find myself needing to know what the fuck he is up to.

So, what do I do? I log right on to my low-key fake page and track him and behold I see that he's out yet again with this lil' Royale' bitch. I don't know why I keep hurting my own damn feelings, because every time I saw the two of them together, it never failed to upset me. It's like, in my heart, I know that seeing him with another woman is a sight I don't ever want to see, but each day, my curiosity was getting the best of me.

I damn near shit myself when I saw him boarding a helicopter with this bitch. Overtaken with anger, I threw my MacBook clear across the room. I broke down with a twisted up, ugly cry face. The aching in my heart was worse than any physical pain I've ever felt. I could feel my torment turning into anger.

Actually, anger is not even the word. It was pure rage. All I could see was red, and I was ready to paint the city the same shade. Once upon a time, I thought I was the baddest bitch in Las Vegas. A bitch couldn't ever tell me that my man would leave me feeling insecure. What the fuck did the bitch have that I don't?

Yeah, she might be cute, but I'm cute too. I've mastered the art of teasing and pleasing his dick, and every now and then, I even throw this man a treat and let him fuck other bad bitches. Kaseeno should feel like a fool for leaving me, but instead, he was out with Royale', and I was the one sitting around crying like a damn fool. There was a time he needed me, and now he didn't even want me. I felt discarded, like a piece of fucking trash.

Fuck that! I wiped my tears and sucked back all the resentment that was building up inside of me. I had to get my shit together, and I had to get it together quickly. I couldn't allow myself to continue sitting around crying over this nigga. I made a vow to myself that I refused to be his victim. Instead, I would seek the retaliation that is rightful mine. Hell has no fury as a woman scorned, and at this point, I want nothing more than to see their newfound relationship burn to the ground, so guess who's going to be the bitch to light the match?

22

Kaseeno

"Baby, it's okay. Bae, I'm here. It's okay."

Royale' was drenched in so much sweat that you would have thought somebody had poured a gallon of water on her. After our night on the town having dinner and going on the helicopter ride, we grabbed a fifth of D'Ussé' and laid out on some plush pillows in the front of my fireplace. I lit a Backwood full of some of the most potent sativa that the dispensary offered and just stared at her splendid beauty as I blew circles of smoke clouds into the air. Midnight had come and gone, yet still, we sat there gazing into each other eyes and conversing about everything under the sun. Who would have known, that past Royale's guarded wall of apprehension, there lied a woman who was so damn easy to talk to. The conversation alone was refreshing.

Royale' looked at me with adoring eyes that made a nigga feel like a king, and she was most definitely a queen to me. No other woman in my past can hold a candle next to shorty. I can't deny that Royale's in a league of her own. It's very rare to encounter a woman with her level of demure and class. There was a godly glow that radiated from her smile, and the more the liquor flowed, the more comfortable she became until she was almost like putty between my fingers.

As Royale' laid on her stomach, I couldn't help but admire the curve that stretched from the small of her back, leading to her ample round ass. I licked my bottom lip, enjoying the view of her shapely body. I threw back the last of my drink and scooted closer to her. My fingers had a mind of their own as they maneuvered across her shoulder blades. I massaged away until I could almost feel the tension leaving her spine. By the time I made it down to that big ole ass of hers, she was as relaxed as a nappy-headed bitch with a fresh perm.

"Damn, that feels so good."

"Yeah? I got something that feels even better."

"Do you?" She was tipsy, and I could see the wheels in her head spinning, so I knew this was the moment I had been waiting for.

"Hell yeah." I pulled my erect dick out of the gray joggers I had changed into, and I watched as the craving filled her pretty brown eyes.

I lifted her sundress above her waist and bit down on my bottom lip. That ass was perfect and smooth, not a single pimple or blemish on it. Her poor little thong didn't stand a chance. I ripped that shit to shreds and dove face-first right into her fat, freshly shaved pussy. Her shit tasted just like strawberry flavored Italian ice on the hottest summer day.

The shit was so good I had to stop myself from busting a nut right then and there. Royale' threw her head back as her long Brazilian inches quickly became disheveled as she enjoyed this moment of pure euphoria. Her mouth formed an O shape as I savored the flavor of her sweet juices. I looked up and watched as her soul left her body. The shit got so good to her that she started to reach for shit that wasn't even there.

"Oh... shit, Mr. Menace," she cried out.

It turned me on whenever she called me Mr. Menace. That shit made a nigga feel like the boss, her boss. I started going even harder, shaking my head all in that pussy until she exploded and came all in my mouth.

Not one to waste a meal, I relished in the excess essence of her wetness. In other words, I was sure to drink every last drop. I basked in the aromatic scent of her pheromones. Fuckin' Royale' was most definitely an experience. While she was busy tryin' to catch her breath and process what just happened, I slapped her on her bare, black ass.

"Bend over."

She wasted no time assuming the position, and I wasted no time diving deep into her guts. Her pussy was so tight that you would have thought that Royale' was a virgin or something. She tried to slither away like a snake. I could tell by the way she was moving that the thick girth of my manhood was killing her lil' ass, but I refused to let that dripping pussy slip away. I pulled her leg back towards me with the quickness.

"Naw, baby, don't run now. Keep that ass still."

I placed my palm down on the arch in her back. At first, I took it easy on her, sliding my dick in and out really slowly. Royale' was enjoying the slow strokes so much that she began to moan seductively and started throwing that ass back and putting that pussy right on me. Once we both caught on to the rhythms of each other's bodies, it was almost like a magical experience. I sped up the pace and started fucking her like this was the last slice of pussy on earth.

"YASSSSS, THAT SHIT SO GOOD, BABY!!!! FUCK!!!! FUCK ME!!!"

The more she talked her shit, the closer I got to busting my nut, and I wasn't ready. I wanted this to last forever. That pussy felt like paradise, and I was working on leaving my mark in it. The type of love that she had was endless, and if I wasn't sure before, now I was damn sure that whatever this was between us was something that I wanted for eternity. I took my last deep stroke and threw all caution to the wind. Fuck it, I busted my nut and rolled over, smiling in exhilaration.

Royale' cuddled up under me, and I welcomingly wrapped my arms around her. You know the feeling you get when you reach a place of tranquility. That's where I was lying next to her. The shit just felt right. I was so content that I fell into a light slumber. I thought that everything was everything until I felt the tremble of her body beneath mine.

It broke my heart to roll over and find Royale' cradled in a fetal position, just crying her pretty brown eyes out. It looked like her whole soul was in pain. I pulled her near as she shivered and sniffed back tears. I hoped that in my embrace, she would know no agony at all. My wish was for my tender love and care to be enough to mend the shattered pieces of her heart. I held her so close to my chest that her cries in the night were muffled.

"Shhhh…Go to sleep, baby."

23

Royale'

"Baby, it's okay. Bae, I'm here. It's okay."

Over the years, I've become accustomed to waking up doused in my own sweat, but this time, things were different. Instead of having one of those horrendous nightmares, I finally had a dream, and instead of being alone, I was wrapped in Kaseeno's arms. After all the years that Remy has been gone, she finally came back and revealed herself to me. I prayed and asked God many nights to bring her back, and she's never come, but tonight she did. I was baffled, confused, and wondering why now.

So many nights, I've laid alone in my own bed longing to see her again. Yet the one night when I'm away from home, lying here with an amazing man she appears to me who was giving me a sense of closure and peace that I've been so desperately seeking since the day she left this earth. To see her again felt so surreal that I was almost disappointed to find myself awoken back to the reality of a world where she no longer resided.

Immediately, when my eyes flew open, I began to cry,

and I couldn't stop my body from shaking. Luckily, I had Kaseeno there to comfort me.

It's been a long time since I've had somebody by my side to care for me during one of my vulnerable moments. Of course, my girl Pri is always there. However, the comfort hits different when it comes from a strong and masculine black man. So many words could be used to describe our date last night. It was perfect. I mean beyond amazing. It was romance at its finest.

I have no regrets, even though I had no intention of giving this good coochie up on the first date. When I'm with this man, I have a feeling of security. The shit just feels so right. I could already tell that this was the beginning of something both special and beautiful. His soothing touch running up and down my spine was enough to usher me into a peaceful slumber.

"HA!!! HA!! HA!!! BURN IN HELL BITCH!!!"

I couldn't have been sleeping for more than an hour or two when I was startled by the sounds of a sinister laugh and the blaring tone of my car's security alarm. Before I could even get my eyes completely open, Kaseeno jumped up and ran to the window. He pulled the shade down and peeked out to see what was going on. His eyes widen, and his jaw dropped. Quickly, he raced to throw on his basketball shorts.

"AW FUCK!!!! THIS BITCH DONE FUCKIN' LOST IT!" he screamed, running towards the door.

I wrapped myself in the quilt we had been laying on and swiftly followed behind him. Nothing could have prepared me for what I saw next. This bitch had thrown a Molotov cocktail through the driver's side window of my car and sped off, laughing and yelling all sorts of obscenities.

I was livid!

"I'M GONE FUCK YOU UP AGAIN WHEN I CATCH YOU!!! STUPID ASS BITCH!!!" I screamed at the top of my fucking lungs, but she was already gone.

Helplessly, I stood there watching the heat waves as the flames started to rise. The scorching temperatures inside the vehicle caused all the other windows to shatter. Kaseeno rushed past me, running full speed back into the house. Fearful that any moment the car would explode, I took a few steps back and tripped over the covers falling flat on my ass and it hurt. I just busted out crying as he ran back out and started hosing the car down with a fire extinguisher. Shit was all bad.

24

Quita

"HA!!!! HA!!! HA!!!" I sped down Route U.S. 50, laughing my ass off. I was pleased. My plan went off without a hitch. It was literally lit, and it served that little bitch Royale' right to see her shit go up in flames.

That's what the bitch gets. After all, she wanted to see sparks fly between her and my nigga right. So, what did I do? I made sure to make motherfuckin' sparks fly for that hoe, and I don't regret it in the least bit. I left her ass standing there big mad. The stunned look on her face was priceless. Kaseeno's dumb ass just stood there looking pathetic as fuck. I was starting to hate that nigga, for real.

Reality was starting to set in that this shit was really over. Even though part of me still loved him and would always miss what we had back when things were good. Deep down, I know that if we were to get back together, things would never be the same. I could never truly forgive him for allowing another bitch to come in between us and ruin what we spent years creating.

A smile spread across my face as I turned on the radio,

the words of Queen Naija's "Karma" spoke perfectly to my situation.

When she said, *"I held you down for the longest, and I was with you through your darkest moments..."* I felt that shit. It's just like a nigga to switch up on his day one for some new pussy, but never in a million years did I ever expect this shit from Kaseeno. I gave him my heart, my soul, and everything within me willingly. I always thought our love was secure and that it would stand the test of time. I had every reason to believe that this was surely a forever thing.

Now I see that I was wrong. For the last almost five years, I've invested so much of myself into him and only him. My whole identity was wrapped up in this man, and now I realized that I have forgotten who I am without him in the process. The fact Kaseeno was everything to me, but I was disposable to him did not sit well with my spirit. Suddenly, the instant gratification that I had been feeling from lighting her shit ablaze became just a fleeting emotion.

Without warning, I burst into tears and begin beating my steering wheel. I had to pull over to the side of the road and gather myself. As I blew snot bubbles into an old McDonald's napkin, my phone rang through the car speaker. It was Tweetie calling to check on me. Her voice sounded groggy like she had just woken up.

"Hey, Qui, you good?"

"Yeah, I'm on my way," I replied, trying to sniff back mucus and conceal my tears, but who was I kidding? Not my best friend, Tweetie, knew me inside and out.

I could hear shuffling as she sat up in bed. She huffed and puffed into the speaker. "What's wrong now? Please don't tell me it's got anything to do with that nigga."

"You already know," I sobbed no longer hiding my pain. I instead allowed the tears to flow like rainfall.

Tweetie sighed. I could tell she was tired of hearing this shit, but just like a true best friend, she asked anyway. "What happened now?"

"I lost it, bitch. I did some crazy ass shit this time, and I don't even care no more. I couldn't fucking help it. They deserve it." At this point, I was damn near hyperventilating.

"Quita, friend, first of all, you have to calm down. Breathe, bitch!" I took her advice and closed my eyes for a half of a minute to catch my breath.

"Now tell me where you are and what the fuck have you done this time?"

"I'm in my car. I went to Kaseeno's house, and he was in there laid up with that bitch. I saw her car parked out front in his driveway, so I filled a Mr. Pure juice bottle with some bleach and stuck a washcloth in it, and I lit the end and threw that shit right through her fucking window."

"Quita, please tell me you not serious right now?"

"Bitch, does it sound like I'm playing?" I said as I began crying again. I could hear her sigh once again out of frustration.

"Aww, man, Qui. You're losing yourself bae for real, and it's starting to concern me. You are acting recklessly without thinking first. Now, what if you had gone to jail, or worse, what if he or that hoe came out shooting and you had lost your life? Ain't no nigga worth that. You don't need his ass bitch, and I'm only telling you this because I love you for real. You got a job, and you already know that as long as I have a place to stay, you are more than welcomed. You got too much going on for yourself to allow Kaseeno to bring you down. Please just bring your ass home and leave his ass alone. If he wanna be with that girl, wish they ass well and move on, friend."

"Fuck that! I'm hurt, Tweetie. I want him to feel it too."

"That's not the answer though. By you constantly doing shit to try to make Kaseeno feel what you feel, all you are really doing is pushing him further away and into the arms of this bitch. You could be investing that energy into something more productive to better yourself. Success and prosperity is always the greatest payback period. Shit, Beyoncé' said it best, your best revenge is your paper."

Damn, as much as I didn't want to hear that, I knew what my girl was telling me was the truth. Hell, she topped her point off with a Beyoncé quote, and she knows I love Queen B. That's why I love Tweetie so much because I can always count on her to always have my best interest at heart. I put my foot on the brake and shifted the gear into drive.

"You right. I was trippin', but I'm good now. I'm on my way. Can you please make me some breakfast?"

"Aiight, I got you, bitch. Now hurry your crazy ass up... out there fuckin' up them people shit." I laughed, wiping the remnants of tears from my cheek. I pressed the button on my steering wheel to end the call and cruised all the way blasting "Formation".

25

Kaseeno

I knew that bitch Quita was crazy, but I had no idea that the hoe was a pyro psycho. A nigga couldn't believe she had the balls to pull a stupid stunt like that knowing damn well that I'm gone fuck her up whenever see her pathetic ass again. I was stuck in a state of bewilderment. I mean, she really caught me off guard. It was the crack of dawn, I hadn't even rolled over, scratched my ass, or gotten the cold out of my eye yet, and here she comes with the bullshit.

Damn, I wish this bitch just move on with her lil' lesbian lover, and hopefully, they can find themselves a new nigga to break them off with some dick. Maybe then, her miserable ass could be happy and leave me the fuck alone. Shit, as far as I'm concerned, this daddy dick belongs to Royale' now. So, while her deranged ass was riding off into the sunrise laughing like the gawd damn joker, I was once again left again to deal with the aftermath of her foolishness. I ran full speed back into the house barefooted with nothing but my basketball shorts on.

Thinking quickly, I grabbed the fire extinguisher, ran

back out, and got on some straight fireman type shit. My poor baby Royale' was so distraught she just sat on the ground and started sobbing. I had to lift my queen back up to her feet and hold her all while apologizing and reassuring her that everything was going to be okay. I held on to her and consoled her until the police arrived to take the report. Because I didn't have an address on Quita, they had no clue where to go to pick her up.

So basically, it seemed like the bitch was free to get away with this shit Scott free, for now, anyway. I know I bet not see her or it's up there, for real. So, it will be best for them to catch her messy ass before I do.

Once the police left, we did too. I figured Royale' would be more at ease back at her place, so we grabbed some food and headed over there.

After we ate, she gathered the police report and all of her insurance information and got on the phone with Geico to handle her business. In the meantime, I got on business, and got my relator on the line. I told them to list my Sumerlin estate as soon as possible. It was officially time for me to move on. Even though the home is where my mother lived after my pops died, it's also the place where I thought I would build a life and have children with that demon bitch Quita. Now that she is a thing of the past, I'm ready to move on and be comfortable without her popping up and fucking up what I got going with Royale'.

THE NEXT MORNING bae went to pick up her rental and was out making the rounds tending to her nail clients. While she was busy doing that, I had a trick or two up under my sleeve. I went to see my homie, Ken, one of the top Porsche dealers at Gaudin of Las Vegas. He promised me a sweet deal if I came back to shop with them again after I bought Quita a truck for her birthday. Since she did that dumb ass shit last night, I figured the least I could do is cop Royale' that all black 2020 Porsche Cayenne coupe with the matching black and red Forgiato rims and if that wasn't enough to lift her spirits and make her smile again, then I had one more surprise in store for her.

I pressed her line. "Wassup, baby? Are you done handling your business for the day?"

"Almost where you at?" Royale' asked.

"I'm bout to send you my location so that you can come slide on me."

"Now, you know I'm working the bar tonight?"

"Shit call off. Who's gone fire you?"

Royale' laughed. "Yeah, alright, nigga. Send the location. You're gone have to give me like an hour though."

"Bet."

26

Royale'

After I serviced my last client, I was prepared to head down to the bar for my shift. Last night's events were crazy, but I still had a bag to get to, and my paper doesn't stop for nothing, not even a deranged ass stalking bitch. This hoe Quita was so pressed, but I'm just like a City Girl...bitch I'll take your man, PERIODT! Just like I took Kaseeno, and I'm not coming up off of him at all. After he laid that bomb ass dick on me, we made things official, and that's my nigga now.

That bitch is just going to have to accept that shit. This morning, I didn't even have to ask, Kaseeno just handed me $2,000 and told me to go get a rental car. I could tell that he was embarrassed that he ever even fucked with this goofball Jamal ass hoe. He kept apologizing relentlessly for Quita's actions, and I had to tell him that it was cool, and that I didn't blame him. I know her ultimate goal is to run me away, but I reassured him that I wasn't going anywhere, anytime soon.

Kaseeno's been texting me all day, and now that I have the evening off, I was headed straight to his location. I don't know what he was doing up in Sheep Mountain, but I'm sure that I would find out once I got there.

I pulled up to a gated community where there was a security station. A young, fat white guy came out and walked to my driver's side window asking for my I.D. I handed it to him and waited as he wrote my name down on his clipboard.

When he was done, he smiled and handed it back to me. I thanked him and waited as he entered his station and pressed the button that opened the gates. All the homes in the community looked expensive. They all had tile roofing, but each one was unique, yet stunningly breathtaking. Each lawn was perfectly manicured, with all the trimmings well-groomed and maintained.

My GPS alerted me that I was approaching the destination that Kaseeno had sent. It was a beautiful single-family home sprawled out over one acre of land. There was a casita, and the courtyard was beautiful, complete with bushes, cactus plants, and palm trees. I parked and dialed Kaseeno's number, but it rang until it went to the voicemail. I was just about to get frustrated, then I saw Kaseeno emerge from the seamless glass door on the patio carrying a dozen long-stemmed roses.

I don't know what was shining brighter, the VVS diamonds on his neck and in his ears or the smile on his face when he saw me get out of my car. Kaseeno kissed me passionately and handed me the flowers. I have to admit that being back in his presence was the highlight of the long day that I had. Somehow, he has this unique way of making me everything feel a million times better, and whenever I'm with him, I feel like the most blessed and beautiful girl in the world. He took my hand and began to lead me toward the house.

"Come on. I got something really special just for you."

We walked up a few stairs and around to the back of the house where there was a long driveway that led to a three-car garage. He pulled a small remote from his back pocket and pressed the button, opening the garage door. Inside, there was a fully loaded black on black 2020 Porsche Cayenne coupe with black and red rims and a matching red bow on the hood. I was so in awe that without thinking, I dropped my Michael Kors handbag and jumped into his arms.

"Oh my god, baby! Thank you so much! I love it. I love you." I gasped, not believing that I had let those words leave my lips. By the look on his face, he was just as surprised as I was.

"Damn, I mean, I didn't wanna move too fast... but shit, since we are being honest, I love you too, bae. Since the moment I first laid eyes on you, I knew, and now that you are mine, I really want this shit forever."

We kissed again, and I damn near wanted to take his sexy ass down right here in this garage, but I was thirsty to take my new car for a spin. I hopped down and opened the door, comfortably adjusting my round ass in the leather seats. Kaseeno looked on dotingly, smiling as I played with the buttons on the steering wheel and opened and closed the sunroof. I flipped through the radio stations and customized it, adding my favorites to the settings. I was all set and ready to go.

"Come on. What are you waiting on? Get in so we can take it around the block."

Kaseeno laughed. "Hold up, bae. It'll be plenty of time for that, but right now, I got another surprise in store for you."

"Really? What in the world could be bigger than this?"

"Come on. You'll see."

He grabbed my hand again. This time he guided me

through a door that led into the spacious home complete with six bedrooms and five and a half bathrooms. It was perfect, with not one single scuff mark on the beautifully laid hardwood floors. The contemporary upgrades included décor paint, stone pattern tile, shutters, high-end cabinetry, and Viking appliances. Everything was so extravagant that I was convinced this had to be the most ravishing residence in all of Nye County.

"Do you like it?"

"Like it? I love it."

"Good, because it's yours...well, it's ours. That's if you agree to move in with me."

"Are you kidding me? I mean... yes. Oh my god, of course, I will. You got me at a loss for words right now," I said, clutching my imaginary pearls.

Kaseeno walked over to me and wrapped his arms around me, pulling me into a hug. I looked up at him and stood on my tippy toes so that I could kiss his sweet lips. I swear nobody has ever made me feel the way his love made me feel. Now I knew what Xscape meant when they sang about the "Softest Place on Earth". This was it. I found love in Paradise, Nevada.

27

Quita

I sat at my desk, and I could barely keep my eyes open. Today was my last day of training, and the first day that I'd be taking live calls. For some reason, my mind felt foggy, and it was making it difficult for me to concentrate on my work. Aside from that, I couldn't wait for lunchtime to arrive. I planned to rush over to Freddy's for frozen custard and one of those bomb-ass steak burgers. The craving was so real that my mouth watered just thinking about it.

It was 12:17 p.m., and I was watching the clock like a hawk. My stomach was doing backflips. I closed my eyes and took a deep breath, hoping that when I opened them again that it would be 12:30 p.m. These were the longest thirteen minutes of my life. Time was moving slower than a snail.

I couldn't take it anymore. At 12:25 p.m., I hit the step away button, to stop my dialer system from spinning any more calls. I got up to excuse myself to the washroom. As soon as I stood to my feet, I felt dizzy, and everything around me seemed like a blur. I felt a little off-balance.

"What's wrong?" Tweetie whispered. I opened my

mouth, but instead of words coming out, I vomited all over the computer screen. I was so embarrassed. My manager rushed over to ask was I okay, but I wasn't.

My equilibrium was all out of sync with the rest of my body, and my knees grew weak beneath me. To sum it up in a few words, I felt like shit. I tried to catch my balance, but my attempt was unsuccessful. I blacked out completely.

WHEN I CAME TO AGAIN, I was on a gurney being rushed to the emergency room at Sunrise Hospital and Medical Center.

The nurse lifted my eyelids one at a time, flashing a flashlight into my pupils. I no longer felt dizzy, but I was still dazed and confused. My mouth was dry, and I was thirsty as fuck. Nurses and nurse assistants swarmed around me. They pushed me into a private room and immediately commenced to hooking me up to an IV.

"Ms. Powell, do you know what city you're in?" One of the nurses asked.

"Vegas," I whispered through my fatigue.

"What year is it?"

"2019."

"Patient is both responsive and coherent," she told her colleagues as she wrapped the blood pressure cuff around my arm. "Try to hold still and remain calm. I'm just going to take your blood pressure. Have you had anything to eat or drink today?" I just shook my head, but I wanted to scream out HELL, NAW! Lord knows I was hungry as hell, and I'd probably be somewhere pigging out right now had I not passed out.

"Your blood pressure is 116/80, not bad. Okay, Ms. Powell," she said, taking off her blue latex gloves, "I'll check with the doctor. He may want to collect some blood from you to run a battery of tests. If so, you'll have to wait a lil' while before you can eat, but in the meantime, we'll put your order in so you can eat immediately after. Do you have any food allergies?"

I shook my head no again, and she handed me a menu. I cleared my throat so that I could speak.

"How long am I going to be here?" I asked. She tilted her head and had a look of compassion upon her face.

"Well, I'm not sure. At least until we find out what caused you to pass out. Now relax. Here, take this remote. Watch a lil' TV. I have to make my rounds but you push this button if you need anything, and I'll be right back with the doctor. He'll know more, okay?" I nodded in agreeance.

"Oh, I almost forgot. Your friend that rode here with you in the ambulance seemed pretty worried about you. She almost wouldn't allow the EMTs to do their job, so we had to ask that she wait in the waiting room. Would you like to allow her to come back now?"

"Yes, please." I murmured.

Tweetie came in with tear stains on her cheeks. Her sensitive ass was really worried about me, and it warmed my heart the way she carried about making sure I was comfortable. She was on the nurses' ass, constantly bugging on them until they brought me a hard ass pillow and a heated blanket. She stayed right by my side, gripping my hand as the nurse's assistant filled four small vials full of my blood. The starving bitch even helped me eat my lunch when they finally brought my tray up. We just laughed and talked shit until the fine ass doctor finally walked in looking like Jay R. Ellis. His charming smile illuminated the entire room.

"Good evening Mrs. Powell."

I sat up and smiled right back, "That is Miss Powell. Dr...."

"Evans. Dr. Charles Evans." He extended his hand, and I shook it.

"It's a pleasure to meet you, Dr. Evans. I mean, I wish it was under better circumstances, of course," I flirted, but he remained professional.

"Yes. Are you feeling a little better?"

"I'm sure she is now that she's under your care." Tweetie must have been reading my mind because she was looking at him like he was a steak on a platter.

"Hush bitch, he wasn't asking you." I cleared my throat and focused my attention back to Dr. Sexy. "Yes, Dr., I think I'll be just fine… like you." He blushed, bashfully, but stuck to the business at hand. He flipped through my chart, and something, in particular, must have sparked his interest because I noticed his eyebrow rise.

"Hmmm..."

I started to get concerned. "Is something wrong, doc?"

"No, not necessarily wrong."

"Then what is it that you're over there looking at?"

"Just the result of the test that we've run."

"Well, what does it say?"

"It says that you're pregnant, six weeks pregnant, to be exact. Congratulations, you're going to be a mom."

28

Kaseeno

Ever since I bought Royale' her new truck and our new home, it seems like our bond has gotten even tighter and stronger. Still, that hasn't stopped Quita from pulling out all the stops to try to get in contact with me. Her latest antic was sending an ultrasound to my inbox on Instagram. Most likely, it was some fake shit she found online somewhere. I didn't even respond. I just blocked her ass and kept it moving.

Royale' had me so busy. Between the constant fucking we have been doing and shopping to decorate our new spot, I definitely don't have the time or patience to deal with shorty's fuckery. Hell, these days, my bae and me had been so wrapped up in one another that neither one of us have even been down to the club for work. That's the benefit of being a boss. Luckily, Vega was done training and back to holding things down on the business front. Not only could I kick back and enjoy my leisure time, it felt good having the power to make sure that my lady can do the same. Today, I got another surprise in store for her.

This time it wasn't anything material. I'm taking her to

a special place where no other woman has been with me, not even Quita. I told her to hurry up and get dressed, and we hopped in her new ride. She just hated that I wouldn't let her in on exactly where we were headed. If it's one thing my baby hates, its surprises.

"How do I even know if I'm appropriately dressed if you won't even tell me where we're going?" Royale' asked, rolling her eyes.

"Baby, trust me. You are fine in whatever you wear."

"Whatever. I still don't know why you can't just tell me."

"Because I already told you it's a surprise."

"And what did I tell you?"

I laughed. "Yeah, yeah... I know you don't like surprises, but daddy been working to change that, right?"

She smiled. "You right."

"Who's right?" I put my hand behind my ear. She knew exactly what I wanted to hear, and it sounded like music to my ears when she said it.

"Daddy."

"You damn skippy."

I whipped into the parking lot of Woodlawn Cemetery. If Royale' was going to truly be the new leading lady in my life, then it's only right that she took this journey with me. I took her hand and helped her walk through the sandy grassland. We passed so many dead flowers and wreaths placed around the different tombstones. All of it mere remnants of the remaining love left on earth after the loss of a loved one that has passed away. When we approached the foot of the monument built in honor of my father, I pulled Royale' close to me and shared with her something that very few people get to see, and that's the vulnerable side of me.

"This is where I come when I need to clear my mind.

This is my family, or at least this is what I have left of them." She snuggled closely under me as we looked down at the names of both my mother and my father.

"What were they like?" She laid her head on my shoulder, and I closed my eyes as I inhaled the refreshing scent of her shampoo, my mind drifted back to my childhood. I smiled.

"My momma, aw man, you would've loved moms... everybody loved her. She was the most fly and demure woman that you could ever meet. Always sleek and very well polished in public like the black Jackie Onassis of Vegas. She used to sit courtside at all my pops fights with her hair freshly permed in one of those French buns, and whatever color fur she rocked, she always had to have a matching handbag and shoes. She'd clap and cheer him on, even when she knew his hoes were in attendance cheering along too. She remained classy at all times and stayed devoted to his philandering ass."

"Damn. I'm sure she didn't deserve that. It sounds like your dad was a real piece of shit... No offense."

I shook my head. "None taken. Pops was a muthafucka, but he was cool. At the end of the day, he was just a man doing the type of shit that young, wealthy niggas do. He could've had any woman in Las Vegas and across the country back then and a lot of them he did have, but he always stayed loyal to moms."

"How is that considered loyalty?"

"Well, because despite his flaws and bouts of infidelity, his main priority was protecting her feelings and his family. He always took good care of home and never brought any kind of scandals her way. He didn't create any outside kids or no shit like that, and those bitches wouldn't dare to ever step to her cause they knew that he would choke snot up out they ass."

"Damn. You're right. His ass was a muthafucka."

"For sho! The bastard was tough, but he taught me everything I know about being a man. I miss them both every day. That's why when you wake up crying in the middle of the night cause you miss your sister, it's almost like I can feel your pain because I know firsthand how it feels to want to be with your people and you can't."

"Do you ever get over it?"

"Nope, but you learn to cope and live with it. You can never replace your family, but one day you'll look you look up and realize that God will place more people into your life that will serve as your family."

"Is that what he did when he sent you?" I looked down at her. In all honesty, I hadn't even thought of that.

"I guess so. As a matter of fact, I know so. As long as you got me, you'll never be alone. That's my word."

"What if there ever come a time where I don't have you?"

"Why would you say that?"

"Because sometimes shit just doesn't work out. Like with you and shorty."

I tilted my head. She was definitely giving me something to ponder on, and there was no denying that she was right. Then again, not every person in your life is destined to stay forever. When I first met Quita, I did think that we'd be together for the long haul. Things don't always go according to our plans.

"You right. Nothing is guaranteed, and as the saying goes, some people are in your life for a season, a reason, or a lifetime. Some people are a temporary fixture in your life, and they're only to help you to transition into your next season. That's what I think happened with Quita. When I met her, I was a different man. I was hurting, and I was broken. Many voids in my life needed to be filled, and she rose to the occasion. I appreciate her for being all that she was to me during those trying times. Her love really saved me and brought me back from a dark place. She didn't allow me to continue to sit around and feel sorry for myself. Instead, she challenged me to face my demons, and that's what you need to do."

"What you mean?"

"It's like fight or flight. I don't think you ever took the time to process all the shit that was happening around you back home. In your weakest moment, you probably felt like you ain't have the strength to stay and fight, so it was easier for you just to take flight."

"Can you blame me?"

"Naw, but the things about those demons is there is no escaping them. They'll follow you wherever you go. You can choose to run if you like, but you'll soon find that until you decide to confront the shit head-on, you'll just spend your whole life running."

29

Royale'

Every passing moment spent with Kaseeno is one that I hold near to my heart and cherished. Never in my past have I ever met a man like him, and something inside me told me that I never would again. He is most definitely one of a kind. Past Kaseeno's good looks, charm, and immeasurable wealth, there lies a wise man that is so profound. Whenever he speaks, I listen so intently because I know there is something to be learned.

I walk away from our conversations, looking at the world through a whole new lens. He was teaching me so much about life and myself. I thank God and his parents for creating him. After our visit to the cemetery, I couldn't help but feel enlightened. For the first time since we've met, I actually got a sense of where he comes from.

Just like me, Kaseeno has experienced significant loss and the pain that comes with it, but unlike me, he has been able to process it all and move on. It was time that I do the same. He was right, my sister's untimely passing reduced me to absolutely nothing. I was so distraught and emotionally defeated that I felt I had nothing left in me to stay in Chicago and fight for my peace or for what little family and love that I had left there. Whenever I even think about home, I think about how alone I felt without my twin, and yeah, the easiest thing for me to do was to walk away and start fresh somewhere else.

I could leave Illinois without ever looking back, but what I couldn't leave behind was the overwhelming emotions, the nightmares, and the depression. I've been so busy running, but somehow, the shame and guilt are never too far behind. The survivor's remorse continually nags at me, and I start to regret my own existence. Like how could I dare go on and feel like I deserve to live a happy life while my sister is not here to enjoy her own? How could I ever be content with knowing that I wasn't there at the time when she needed me the most?

A part of conscience reminds me that there was nothing that I could have said or done to help her, but still, I feel convicted that I wasn't even present to try. Days have turned into weeks, weeks have turned into months, and the months have turned into years, and still, I haven't come to terms with the entire ordeal. The therapy has failed to change my lingering thoughts and emotions and overworking myself has only proven to be a temporary solution. It wasn't until after my talk with Kaseeno that I realized that if I want a different solution, I have to take a different course of action. So, with God on my side and with the love and support of my man right here by my side, I'm casting away all my doubts and fears today, and I'm boarding a flight from McCarran International Airport straight to O'Hare International.

It's time to stop running and fight. It's time for me to find myself again, the pieces of me that I abandoned and left broken back in Chicago. It's time for me to reclaim every bit of joy that the devil stole from me that night. I imagine the journey won't be easy, but I'm sure it'll be worth it.

As the plane ascended into the air, I closed my eyes and took a deep breath. Almost as if he could read my mind, Kaseeno grabbed hold of my hand and held it tightly.

I held my head up and opened my eyes. This time when I smiled, it was genuine and not forced. When I count my blessings, I count him twice because if it hadn't been for Kaseeno's presence in my life, I wouldn't even be on this quest. I gazed out of the window at the clear blue skies and the cluster of puffy white clouds in the air until I drifted off into a light nap.

AFTER THREE HOURS and fifty-two minutes, we finally landed in the Windy City. After collecting our things from baggage claim, we headed outside the terminal to wait for our Uber ride to take us to pick up the rental car. The crisp autumn air was a change from the scorching heat on the west coast. As the driver made her way down Mannheim Road, I could see where the once green falling leaves were now different shades of red, yellow, and orange. I was finally home, and I was no longer scared, to be honest. In fact, I was excited. After dropping our bags off at the Air BnB, we stopped to eat and then headed over to the florist.

I spared no expense on the most beautiful arrangement of dried white roses that spelled out the name *REMY*. I also bought a balloon on a stick that said *I Love You Sister*. For the first time since the burial, I entered Forest Home Cemetery in Forest Park and followed the road until I was within walking distance of where my sister had been laid to rest. A lone tear fell from my eye as I sat the flowers and the balloon down in front of her headstone. I could feel Kaseeno's gentle caress down my back. I wanted to turn and run away crying, but I would hear his voice as he whispered in my ear.

"It's time now, baby. Everything that you've held bottled up inside that precious heart of yours, it's time for you to pray about it and leave it right here."

Kaseeno grabbed my hand, and we bowed our heads as I cleared my throat choking back the tears that threatened to fall. I paused for a second, searching my heart for the words I wanted to say, and finally, they came.

"Father God, in the mighty name of Jesus, I come to you so humbly not in the spirit of grief or sorrow but with a heart full of Thanksgiving. I thank you, Lord, for this day and for the strength to return to this place. Thank you for your grace and for your love that has kept me. Thank you for the love you have sent that abounds me. Thank you, for I know that the peace that you are giving me is right on the horizon. Forgive me for my sins, for I am an imperfect creature. Forgive me because when Remy left, my heart hardened, and I question you so many times because I could not understand how you could allow me to hurt so bad God. I now know that it was all a part of your will, and nothing happened that you did not allow. Forgive me, father, but also allow me to forgive myself. Lord, I didn't know all that she was going through here on earth, but what I do know is Remy is now safe in your arms far from the grasp of any harm. Now, I ask that you bless me with a renewed strength and deliver me from the guilt and pain so that I may live a life filled with the abundance and prosperity that you promised me, God. These and all other blessings we ask in your son Jesus' name. Amen."

"Amen."

Kaseeno released my hand and pulled me close into a hug, and I began to wail into his chest. The tears I cried were no longer tears of suffering. It felt like a purging or release. I stayed there in the safety of Kaseeno's arms and let it all out. Finally, I felt like it was okay to truly move on. After a while, I let him go, and I was preparing to walk away and leave. I saw something in the distance that caught my eye.

A woman was approaching. She was dressed in all black with the gusty winds carrying her long flowing shirt. She held on to the top of her hat that was so big that it covered half of her face. Although she was shrouded in mystery, there was still something very familiar about her. Just when I started to walk away and disregard it, I felt Kaseeno's strong grasp holding me there.

"Wait! Look."

Kaseeno nodded towards the woman who was getting closer and closer with every step. I squinted in hopes that I could get a better view. Now, she just a few feet ahead, and my jaw dropped. There she stood, in the flesh, right before my eyes and I couldn't believe it. She outstretched her arms, and I dropped my handbag and ran the short distance to her.

"OH MY GOD! MAMA!" My tears became hers as we embraced each other for what felt like forever.

"Royale'. My baby, I'm sorry. I'm so, so sorry for everything. I'm sorry, baby." She just kept apologizing, but in my heart, I already forgave her. Taking her hands into mine, I stood back and examined her from her head to her toes.

My mom was nothing like I remembered when I last saw her. She was clean. She had even picked up some weight and looked to be very healthy. Of course, she was older. The fine lines and slight wrinkles were only a testament to the hard time that she had spent on the street.

Still, she was beautiful, just like she had been in all the old photographs that my granny had kept.

"It's okay, ma. I promise it's okay."

"No, I have to say this. I should have been there for you. I should have been there for Remy, but I didn't know how. I didn't know how to be a good mother to y'all when I couldn't even be a good woman for myself. I was lost baby, I was so lost, and when you found me and asked me to come with you, I was so scared. I know you think I left you hanging, but I didn't. I was there that day, and I saw you waiting, and you looked so broken, baby. You looked like you needed someone, someone who could be strong for you, and I couldn't. I couldn't be strong. I couldn't be what you needed in that moment because I was broken too. I'm sorry because I wasn't ready, baby. I wasn't prepared, and the last thing I wanted was to become a burden for you or to hurt you more. So, I just ran. I ran away before you could see me, and I spent so much time after that, just running.

I thought about you every day. I prayed that you were safe, and every day, I regret not leaving with you. I'm sorry, and I'm here, and I'm not running anymore, and if you let me, I promise I'll never run again. I vow to always be here for you. I love you, baby."

Tears slowly fell from my eyes because she was baring her soul and spilling her heart out to me with all sincerity. I never knew that she was there that day, and of course, I needed her then. Hell, I still do. I understand that back then, she was battling her own demons, and it wasn't her fault that she couldn't be there when I felt I had no one else and terribly needed someone to be there to hug me and tell me that things were going to be alright. Even if things weren't truly going to be alright, it would have been nice to have my mother there to console me, but she wasn't there, and I can't change the past.

I swallowed deep and hard. I paused for a moment and looked into her eyes. They were filled with sorrow. Her pupils were filled with wasted years and regret. What else did she truly have? Here she stood at the foot of her daughter's grave, pleaded for forgiveness.

There was nothing I could have said or done to help her back then, but today was a new day. This wasn't one of those dreadful nightmares. She was really here after all this time. I can't change the past, but I could make it my business to look towards a brighter future for both of us. I know that's what Remy would have wanted.

I wiped my eyes and hugged her again. "I love you too, ma. I swear. You're here now, and that's all that matters to me. We can finally start over and be a family. Forget everything that happened. Let's just look towards all the amazing times to come. I'm ready to create some great memories with you lady, so get ready. PERIODT!"

She chuckled at my ratchetness and looking at her smile gave me a pleasant sense of relief. I don't know how to explain it. It's like, this was a moment that we both had dreamed of, but I never knew if it's would ever actually happen in real life. We hugged it out for like two minutes straight. It's like time stood still, and for a moment, it felt like we were the only ones there.

I was so focused on loving her and being loved by my mother that I had damn near forgotten that Kaseeno was there until he cleared his throat. We let go of each other, and this time, I was the one apologizing.

"I'm sorry. Kaseeno, this is my mother, and ma, this is my man Kaseeno." I stood back and watched as she walked around me and embraced him.

"I know who he is. Come here, son. Thank God for

you, young man. Thank you for being such a good man, being there for my daughter, and for helping me out. I truly appreciate it, and none of this would be possible without God sending you."

I looked on confused.

"I'm sorry, but did I miss something."

"Royale', I had been trying to get clean by myself for so long and for a while it would work, and then I'd be right back getting high, but about a month ago, some people reached out to me, and they said they knew where you were. They gave me Kaseeno's number, and he promised me that he would help me to reunite with you, but first, he made me promise that I would get myself together, and I did. He told me that he would help me and true to his word he sure enough did. He put me in a 30-day program where I went through groups and individual therapy. He paid for my doctor's visits and everything, and when I got out, he made sure I had clothes, a place to stay, and whatever I needed. I couldn't have done any of this without your help, man. I swear, I owe you so much."

"You don't owe me a thing, ma'am. I did that because it was on my heart to. In fact, if anything, I owe you for giving birth to this amazing woman that's captured my heart in so many ways. Just to see her smile and reunite with her family is all the payback I'll ever need."

I smiled. Kaseeno had planned all of this without me having the slightest clue. This entire trip had been his idea, and every time I felt any apprehension, he would ease my mind and push for me to go through with it, and I'm glad he did. My man had become the king of surprises, and it's like each time he outdoes himself. Kaseeno's love for me surpasses anything I ever felt in the past and to know that it runs so deep that it's beyond just me, but it extends to my family.

That shit warmed my heart in a way that words can't even begin to explain. It's crazy how even when you're not looking and when you least expect it, love will meet you right where you are even in the midst of all your bullshit. God truly blessed me when he sent Kaseeno into my life, and if it is His will, I want this love to last a lifetime.

30

Quita

It was finally the end of the month and my last workday of the week. Honestly, I couldn't wait for this shit to be over so that I could just go home, kick my fat swollen feet up with a big bowl of cookies and cream ice cream and sulk in my misery. This pregnancy and the stress of meeting my quota was kicking my ass. As it turns out, collecting debts isn't as easy as I had anticipated that it would be. For the past week and a half, it seems every debtor I make contact with either hangs up during the mini-Miranda, curses me out, or a combination of both.

If I do get someone polite on the line, who isn't a total bum, they just apologize for being too broke to pay. This shit was for the birds, and I had far too much on my plate and my mind. From day-to-day, it was becoming harder and harder to focus. After my fainting incident, I had taken a couple of days off to regroup and adjust to my new life as an expecting mother. My bosses have been very understanding and even pro-rated my goal for the month, but I was still struggling to hit my number.

Tweetie was even trying to help by giving me some of

her post-dated payment arrangements. I have to say that throughout everything that I had been going through recently, she has been my biggest support system, even catering to me hand and foot at home and making late-night trips to the gas station to get me pickles or whatever else I had urgent cravings for.

Initially, I contemplated having an abortion. My situation with Kaseeno has been complicated enough lately, and the last thing I felt I needed was to add a baby to the mix. My mind was damn near made up, but it was Tweetie who convinced me that this baby was a blessing and reminded me that if I kept it that I was guaranteed to stay in Kaseeno's pockets for at least another eighteen years, and that's all the persuasion I needed to keep it.

Maybe this baby is God's way of helping me cash out. In fact, if it's a boy, I think Kash is the perfect name. CHA-CHING! My bitch just might be on to something. If the worse came to worse, she promised me that she would always be here for the baby, and that gave me an extra boost of reassurance.

For the past couple of weeks, we both began to become excited about the reality of having a new life arriving soon. Although, Tweetie's baby fever was at one hundred-degree Fahrenheit. I laughed at her crazy ass when she came to me with her very own godmother contract. I signed it for shits and giggles, after all, who else would assume that role in my baby's life? I don't have any other girlfriends. Plus, she was already buying my baby hella shit.

When we go into different stores, I can't keep her out of the baby section, and it seems like every other day, there is a shipment at our door from Amazon containing baby rattles, a bassinet or stroller, and even baby clothes. The crazy thing is, it's still very early in the pregnancy, and we don't even know the gender yet. I want a boy, but Tweetie swears up and down that I'm carrying her goddaughter. Every day she's been coming to my desk during her some point of the day asking the same question. "Qui... Are you sure that you don't want a baby shower?"

"Very sure, and I wish you wouldn't ask me again, friend." To me, the whole ordeal was embarrassing. "I don't even have any close family, and you're my only friend."

"Well, what about Karen in Admin and Willie and Liz? We could invite them!"

I shot her a mean look. "Our managers and support staff, Tweetie? Really? I got an idea..." Her face lit up with a glimmer of hope, as if after several days, maybe now I would finally give in and say yes.

I was miserable enough as it is. The last thing I want is to be fat and alone faking a smile and pretending to be happy as I entertain guest that are probably wondering where the child's father is. They would probably ask.

"How about you go back to your desk and call me. I'll patch Karen, Willie, and Liz in on a conference call, and we can do the baby shower like that," I said in my fake customer care voice.

"That baby is making you evil, but whatever. It's above me now." She threw her hands up into the hair as she turned around and strutted her stuff back to her desk.

I'd rather spend my Saturday home in bed eating Popeyes and lurking on the Gram than be out in public at a dry ass baby shower. Then again, maybe I should allow her to throw it and invite my trifling ass baby daddy so that we could celebrate the wealth that he would soon be losing and that my baby and I would now gain. He better know that I'm about using this opportunity to take his bitch ass straight to cleaners and milk him for every last dime in his pocket.

I reached out to his womanizing ass on Facebook and messaged him a picture of my ultrasound. The very first picture of our baby. You would think, after years of always telling me that one day I'd have his kid, he would at least have the decency to put his arrogance aside and respond. Wishful thinking, I guess. That nigga just viewed the message and blocked me. That shit was like a slap in not only my face but in the face of our unborn child as well. I know I haven't been the friendliest or the easiest person to deal with in the last few weeks, and I have done some pretty foul shit, but despite all of that, I didn't make this baby by myself.

This child has done no wrong to him or no one else. My baby never asked to be here, but whether Kasseno likes it or not, this baby is coming, and I refuse to let anyone hurt my child. Nobody better try mine, not even my hoe ass baby daddy. When I saw that he blocked me, I had to close my eyes and breathe deep. Everything in me wanted to spazz out and do some more crazy shit, but now I had more to think about than just myself.

Although it was easier said than done, I had to stop myself from feeling infuriated. I could already feel my blood pressure trying to rise, and the doctor already warned me to keep my stress levels down. If I thought too long on all the wrong that's been done to me, I would be liable to go down a crazy path and do something destructive, and I couldn't have that right now. I adjusted my thoughts and focused on more positive energy, like the new life growing in my womb. That was enough to shift my mood and make me smile again.

The baby must have felt my heart flutter a bit because I was shocked to feel a tiny kick. I stroked my belly as my eyes widened will joy. It felt weird but in a good way. In that moment, I had an epiphany, and something inside of me changed for the better. I think it finally hit me, the reality that in only a matter of months, I would be responsible for bringing a whole new life to the earth.

Just the thought made me a little nervous, but there was no turning back now. Next week I'd be entering into my second trimester, and I'm going to be somebody's mama. This was happening, and I made a conscious decision that come hell or high water I am going to be the best damn parent that this child would have. Hell, as far as I'm concerned, I'm the only parent this baby has, which means I got to go extra hard, and I know it probably won't be easy, but I'm ready to accept the challenge.

Never would I have imagined that my broken heart could be stolen by a tiny individual who wasn't even on earth yet, but that's exactly what has happened. I already wanted to give this baby everything good in the world, including two parents. Despite what has transpired in my soul, I still love Kaseeno. When I think about the amazing gift he has left inside of me, I forget all the anger and rage that I had felt since he left me. My heart softened, wondering if I should wave the white flag and attempt to reach out once more.

Maybe I overreacted. After all, we went half on this baby, and taking the journey to parenthood is something that neither of us has yet to experience. This would be his very first child, and I don't want to rob him of the opportunity to be there for all the baby's most important moments. Sure, he had not been the perfect man for me, but at this point, this shit is bigger than me. So, I promised myself that I would reach out and apologize and try to come to a reasonable solution for the sake of my baby.

WHEN I GOT HOME that evening, I showered, ate a fat ass Quesarita from Chipotle, and tuned in to the Investigation Discovery Channel. Tonight, they were airing a marathon of my favorite show, *Snapped*. It's crazy because I used to watch this show and think that the murderous spouses were all just lunatics, but after my recent break-up with Kaseeno, I watched tonight's episode with a brand new perspective. In the words of Amy Winehouse, love is a losing game, and it can push you to the edge in a way that will make one snap and kill. In the past, I had never been hurt, so I couldn't fathom how anyone could ever harm a person that they once vowed to love, but now I understand how rapidly love can turn to hate.

Even though I despised Kaseeno, I still couldn't help but to always think about him. It wasn't long before I found myself page watching once again. As I scrolled down Royale's page, I saw that she had posted some new pictures with him in them. They had taken a trip back to her hometown in Chicago. She was singing his praises and expressing how much she loved him and appreciated him for helping her to reunite with her mother after ten years.

I just shook my head at the images of the three of them huddled and hugged up like a happy family. The shit didn't even look right. He looked out of place. If you ask me, he didn't belong there in this picture with this girl and her moms, especially considering that he is supposed to be here with us, his unborn child and me.

We are his real family, not her. She just came along out of nowhere. For weeks, I been trying to tell myself that all of this was just temporary and that somehow, he would just snap out of it and end this little fling he was carrying on with this lil' hoe, but something about this pictures told me that I was wrong and that was beginning to be more than just a fling.

When I read her comments, everyone was congratulating her on reunited with her old lady and sending them well wishes. One comment, in particular, stood out to me. It was from Priyanka Davis. I remembered that name from when I looked Royale' up. Priyanka was the only name listed as a relative for her in the Las Vegas area.

Priyanka Davis: *Oh my god!!! This is so beautiful, friend. S/o to my bro Kaseeno. You must have been so surprised. I already know you cried like a baby. I'm so happy for you guys. Bring your mom back to Vegas. I can't wait to meet her. Love you, babes.*

Royale' DaNailQueen Lee: *Thank you, bestie!!! I love you more. This man of mine never ceases to amaze me. I cried like a baby and messed up a perfectly beat face. But I'm so happy right now and proud of my mom. We'll be back on Friday, and she's coming with us. I'll call you as soon as we land.*

I stared at the hours and minutes in the corner of my computer screen. Time was moving like a snail, and at this point, I didn't even give a damn about these debtors or their outstanding balances. I couldn't wait to get off and get to my phone. The first thing I planned to do was log into Facebook and both of their pages to see had they made it back into town. Checking on them and tracking their pages was becoming more than a hobby to me.

Slowly but surely, it was becoming an obsession. It was the first thing I did when I awoke in the morning. It was what I did during my lunch hour and the last thing that I did at night, and I wasn't ashamed and didn't feel bad about it. Kaseeno is more than just my boyfriend or my ex. He's my child's father now, and it's my job to know what's going on with him. For that reason, I intend to continue keeping a watchful eye on not only Kaseeno but also the company he's been keeping.

31

Kaseeno

Them hoes ain't fuckin' with you on your worst day
  I got you on a new level like what Ferg say
  When you fell down, I pick you up
  Put on your crown, and lift you up
  I put a rock all on your finger,
  so much ice could push a puck

WATCHING ROYALE' reunite with her mother almost made a nigga want to shed tears of joy, but of course, a nigga like me is too player to be showing emotions. Instead, I looked on pleased that I was able to pull a few strings and make this happen for my lady. There is no love on earth greater than a mother's love. Every single day for the last four years, I have longed to have my mama back, but it won't ever happen, but being able to make that happen for Royale' left me with a feeling of gratitude.

Spending the last couple of days in Chi-Town with Royale' and Ms. Rita was fun. After the tearful reunion at the cemetery, I think we all needed a little pick me up, and since it was my first time being in the city, my girls took me on a tour of the Windy City. We did everything, from the Ferris wheel at Navy Pier to the big bean. I even got the chance to overlook the world from the top of the Willis Tower, or should I say the Sears Tower. That's what bae calls it even though they changed the name of it ten years ago; true die-hard Chicagoans still call it that.

Nevertheless, I never felt so high up in my life. As I looked down over all the amazing architecture that composed the city's skyline, I reflected on what brought me here in the first place. Royale', this beautiful woman that I have known for such a short amount of time, has come into my life and wiggled her way into my heart so swiftly. When we met, my intention wasn't to wife her up, but here I was, 1,450 feet in the sky, honestly considering proposing marriage. Usually, that type of commitment would scare a man, but somehow in this moment, I had no fear.

I guess it's true what they say. When you find your true soul mate, you just know. In some of my past relationships, I thought I was in love. Hell, with Quita, I was sure of it, but with the wild and carefree lifestyle that she led, I still maintained an inkling of doubt. However, this time, there was no question.

Not only was Royale' bad as hell, but she also has ambition and drive that is unmatched. I never met a female that hustles just as hard as I do. My baby is so dope with a fat ass and alluring personality. Seeing her smile today, it's like she's an entirely different woman than she was just a few weeks ago. I gazed at her while she and her mother stood at the window and overlooked the streets below.

She had come to me alone and broken, but at the same time, she was brave. Courageously, she bared her broken heart with me and trusted me enough to share with me her life experiences. She made it so easy for me to want to care for her, but more than that, she also helped me to finally acknowledge my own grief and finally do the work to process it.

As if she could feel my gaze from across the room, Royale' looked up and over in my direction and blushed when she caught me admire her and all of her awe. Man, I can't wait to get her ass back to the hotel suite. I'm going balls deep in it. Fuck it, she's getting a baby put in her tonight.

As she and Ms. Rita walked over towards me, I was hypnotized by the sway of her full hips. I licked my lips, anticipating the next moment that we will have alone. I plan to taste and devour that pussy.

32

Royale'

I don't know what the hell got into Kaseeno, but baby after we left the Sears Tower and got to our hotel suite, he threw me down on the bed and ate my kitten like it was a turkey on the third Thursday in November. He then proceeded to split me wide open with the thick girth of his manhood. The way he pounded in and out of my gushing pussy had me hurting so good that I was thanking the heavens above and begging for mercy at the same damn time. When he startled nibbling on my ear and talking shit, I couldn't take it anymore. I came so hard and squirted everywhere. The shit was so wet and freak nasty that he ain't have no other choice except to cum all up in me.

Usually, when we fuck, Kaseeno always pulls it out, but we both were so caught up in this fuck session that neither one of us wanted to stop. I rolled over and just stared at him, panting hard to catch my breath a euphoric feeling overtook me. I smiled, looking at his sexy ass body lying next to me, and I just shook my head. He bit on his bottom lip and looked back at me with questioning eyes.

"What?"

"You know what, nigga. You ain't even tell me you were cumming."

"You wanted to taste it, didn't you? With your nasty ass."

I smacked in with the pillow, and we both laughed and wrestled butt naked between the sheets. That dick was so good that I threw all caution to the wind. This is my man, and if he wanted to nut all in this good coochie at this point, I wasn't gonna stop him. His ass is so sexy I just shrugged.

"Fuck it. You look like you'll be a good father," I teased. He picked up the pillow and threw it at me, but I playfully blocked it as our giggles continued to fill the atmosphere.

"I hope I put a baby in you too, since you talking shit." He got up and went into the bathroom to run us a bath.

TWO MONTHS Later

Life is great, to say the least. Since returning to Vegas from Chicago, I was happier than I think I've ever been, and finally, I had something that I always wanted, a family. Kaseeno and I spared no expense on furnishing our new home, and we agreed that it would be best if my mother came back to Las Vegas and moved in with us. It's been so much fun hanging out with her and just doing the type of things that mothers and daughters do. She has even taken a liking to my best friend Priyanka, so the three of us are always out shopping and pampering ourselves, and today was no different.

"Oh, look at this one." Priyanka held up the Gucci Zumi bag. I checked the price tag and damned near spit out the complimentary champagne.

"Four thousand, three hundred dollars, bitch? I think not."

"Shit, you can afford it."

"I know, but I'm not about to drop that kind of money on a damn purse. Shit, that can be a down payment on my nail spa."

"True, but I ain't say you had to spend your money on it," she said, giving me a sneaky little look, and I know what she was thinking.

"Aw hell naw. I am not trying to hear Kaseeno's mouth. Put that back." I felt my phone vibrating in my jacket pocket. "Speaking of the damn devil," I said as I answered for my man.

"Wassup, babe?"

"Hey. Where y'all at?"

"Shopping, why wassup?"

"Nothing much, I just miss you, and I wanna take you somewhere special tonight that's all."

"Aww baby. What do you have in mind?"

"It's a surprise. You know how I do."

"Yeah, I already know. Shit is always a surprise."

"And you always end up smiling."

"True. I'm not complaining at all. So, I'll see you later."

"Cool....aye!"

"Wassup bae?"

"Buy you and your mama something nice on me. You deserve it."

"I love you!" I blushed.

"I love you more. See you later, babe."

The champagne I was sippin' already had me a little tipsy, and now Kaseeno had me feeling some type of way. By now, you would think I'd be used to him spoiling and loving on me, but after years of being alone, I'm just getting used to the constant love and affection. I could wait for this little date night, but more than that, I can't wait to get his ass back home and make sweet love. I must have been cheesing and blushing extra hard because both my momma and Pri were looking at me all weird and shit as I picked up the handbag she had just shown me.

"Um, hum! What he say?"

"I deserve it. Excuse me..." I called out to the retail specialist. "I'll take two of these, please. One for myself and my mother. Thanks!"

33

Kaseeno

Tonight would be the kind of night that separates boys from men. I had multiple surprises in store for Royale'. My plan was already in motion, and with the help of Ms. Rita and Priyanka distracting her, my baby didn't have the slightest clue on what was about to go down. Still, I can't lie. I'm both nervous and anxious. My hands trembled as I stared down at the 1.4-carat princess cut diamond ring. I've never asked a woman for her hand in marriage, but tonight I'd be asking Royale' if she would do me the honor of becoming Mrs. Menace.

"It's beautiful, Kaseeno. I'm sure she'll love it," my jeweler. Avianny broke me out of the trance that had engulfed me.

I smiled. "Yeah, I think so too. Thanks, man!"

We gave each other dap. "Oh, it's my pleasure, brother. You've been a loyal customer for many years, and I know that this is a big moment for you. We here at Avianny Jewelers are happy to be a part of that."

This sounded like a script he had repeated many times before, but it was still beautiful to hear.

"I appreciate it. So, you know what to do. Send the invoice over to my assistant, and I got you."

He polished off the rings, put it in a velvet box, and chuckled a bit with that Italian wise guy tone. "Invoice? Really Kaseeno? Don't insult me. What kind of guy do you think I am, man? A jerk off?"

"Huh?" I looked at him, confused. This had been the procedure for most of our transactions.

"This one my friend is on the house. Capiche?"

I threw my head back in awe. I have indeed been shopping with Avianny since my teenage years. He had been my father's jeweler even before that. Still, his kind display of generosity warmed my heart in a major way. We dapped it up once again, and I headed out to prepare for this special night.

34

Quita

I wand curled my Brazilian body wave wig and put on a cute outfit that I had recently ordered from Fashion Nova. Since breaking up with Kaseeno, my days of Gucci and Maison Margiela were over. Although I still had the old designer clothes that he had bought me, because of my growing belly, I could no longer fit into them. So, I had to settle for Fashion Nova. Luckily, I got a pretty face and the kind of ass that make any outfit look good. As I ran the wide-tooth comb through my beautiful tresses, Tweetie appeared from behind the bathroom door, startling me.

"Where the hell are you going all dressed up, bitch?" I almost jumped out of my body at the sound of her voice.

I laid my hand across my chest, feeling my pounding heart. "Oh my god, girl... don't ever scare me like that."

Tweetie looked at me with inquisitive eyes, waiting for me to answer her question. I got nervous because I know once I tell her my plan to visit Kaseeno, she is going to catch a major attitude. Ever since our breakup, Tweetie and I have been fucking more and more, and while she has been my greatest support system in these difficult times, she can't be a father to my child.

That's a role that only Kaseeno can fill.

Somehow, I know that this conversation is going to lead to an argument. So, I swallowed hard and made an effort to choose my words wisely. "Um, I.... well we... me and the baby..."

"Bitch, why are you stuttering? Spit it out."

"I'm going to see Kaseeno."

She chuckled and shook her head. "You just don't quit, do you? That nigga doesn't want you, and I'm sure he doesn't want that fucking baby either."

"Well, he shouldn't have laid down and with me and made it. He has no choice. He might do me wrong, but he's gone step up and be a father to my child. I'm not gone to have it any other way."

"Whatever. Do whatever you gone do bitch, but when that nigga dog your ass again just know I don't want to hear that shit cause at this point, you bringing that hurt on yourself!" Tweetie yelled with a bad attitude and walked away.

I closed my eyes and exhaled. The last thing my big pregnant ass wanted to do was argue with her ass. I made a mental note not to give that bitch any more of this super gushy, pregnant pussy because it was going in her mouth and straight to her head. How dare she scream at me because I was going to go have a conversation with my baby daddy? Who in the hell does this bitch think she is?

Fuck it! I thought, once again, convincing myself not to get all worked up. This baby is really changing me, and I had more to think about than my own emotions. I logged on to Facebook and hit the search button. I have to track this nigga down if I'm going to pop up on his ass.

His page held no clues of his whereabouts. So, I opted

for the next best thing. I checked Royale's page. Most likely wherever he was, that thirsty bitch isn't too far behind. I pressed play on the live video that she had posted from forty-eight minutes ago. She was in the Gucci store with Priyanka and her momma, sippin' champagne and showing off the new purse that "her man" had bought her.

It was the same bag that I had my eye on and had planned to purchase prior to him getting on my ass about what his stupid ass accountant had shown him. All hopes of remaining calm flew right out of the window. I tried breathing deeply just like they taught in the Lamaze class that Tweetie and I had attended last week, and surprisingly, the technique seemed to be working until something familiar caught my eye. As Royale' twirled the purse around showcasing it in front of the camera, I saw it.

Kaseeno signature dice were tattooed on her wrist. Almost instantly, a sense of rage and envy engulfed me. I allowed this bitch to have my man. Royale' had a beautiful home that should have belonged to me, and she had the purse that I so desperately desired, but none of this was enough. She just had to have my fucking tattoo too.

If I didn't know any better, I'd say this bitch was trying to be me. What's next? Will she try to take my baby? Oh hell naw, I lifted my big ass off that couch and waddled over to my closet and removed the shoebox where I stash my Beretta.

I loaded the clip and placed the gun in a hidden compartment in my outdated Gucci purse. I paced the floor back and forth. Tweetie was right. I was bringing all of this emotional trauma onto myself. Every time I tried to be rational, this nigga was out doing something that he knows would ruffle my feathers.

This shit has to end, and it could only end one way. I have to kill this bitch. If not for myself, for my child. I can't continue to allow this bitch to have everything that belongs to me, and who knows, maybe with her out of the picture, Kaseeno will see that with me and my baby is where he should be. I took one more deep breath and put my plan into motion.

35

Kaseeno

My barber put the last finishing touches on my lining, and he had a nigga looking real crispy. Once Royale' lays eyes on her surprise and sees me dripped out in my three-piece suit on bended knee, she will have no choice but to accept this ring. I nodded, looking in the mirror, pleased with my amazing appearance. I paid for my haircut and proceeded to the car when I felt my phone vibrating. The number on the screen was one that I didn't recognize.

My curiosity got the best of me, so I answered. "Hello."

"Kaseeno, I know you saw my message. This is not a game. I'm having your baby, and you're sitting here ignoring me while you in and out of town with this bitch."

I took exhaled in frustration. Just the sound of Quita's voice annoyed the fuck out of me. It was just like her ass to call me and ruin a perfectly good day. Yeah, I had seen her lil' message and chose to ignore her messy ass just like I wished I had ignored this fucking call. Truthfully, I don't think she's pregnant, and if she is, then I pray to God that the baby ain't mine. I ain't fucked her since her birthday, and who knows, with the way she and Tweetie gets down, I wouldn't be surprised if they done found some new dick to bounce on.

"Listen, Quita. Today is not the day. I don't wanna be bothered. You've been running around here doing all that crazy shit, setting fires and all that. You lucky the police ain't caught up with your deranged ass. You better hope they catch you before I do or...."

"Or what, Kaseeno? What? What you gone do? Hurt me? The mother of your first and only child?" She was milking this lil' pregnancy shit for all it was worth, and honestly, all I wanted was for her ass to go away and leave me the hell alone.

"So, you pregnant, for real?" I asked, trying to decipher if this was another one of her desperate attempts to seek attention.

"Yes, Kaseeno, and it's hard carrying this child alone, especially since I'm carrying all of this hurt and resentment that you left me with," her voice softened, and I could tell she was fighting back the tears.

"Look, shit didn't work out. People break up. Shit happens. It's not my fault or your fault, and I'm not about to sit back and apologize for moving on, and I'm damned sure not about to allow you to continue to disrespect my lady."

"Your lady? Really nigga? I just sat back and told you that I'm carrying your child, and all you can worry about is this bitch? You got me fucked up."

"Naw, you got yourself fucked up. You can't accept the fact that I don't want you anymore. I've been told you that I moved on and I'm happy. I want nothing to do with you. We are not going to ever be together again. That shit is so dead. So, it ain't too late to have an abortion."

That last statement must have really hurt Quita's feelings because she went from being confrontational to weeping and sobbing like a child does when they catch a temper tantrum.

"How could you? I was always there for you, and now you can't be here for me, and worse than that, you expect me to kill our child. No, I won't do that. I can't!"

I admit that a part of me felt bad for her, and she was right. She had been there for me during one of my darkest moments. There was a time when I loved the shit out of Quita, and even though that time is in the past, maybe I was being too hard on her right now. I may be a bit of an asshole sometimes, but one thing I can never be is a deadbeat. I rubbed my temple, feeling a headache coming along.

All of this couldn't have come at a worse time. On the hills of my engagement to Royale', I find out that I'm about to be a father. Damn! All I could think about was the negative effect that this news could have on my new relationship. If my girl finds out, this could potentially ruin everything good that we got going on. There has to be a happy medium, a way that I can keep Quita quiet and continue to have my happily ever after with Royale'.

"What do you want me to do, Quita?"

"At this point, I just want you to step up and be a man Kaseeno. What do you think you should do?"

I didn't quite know the answer to that question, but what I do know is there is nothing a few dollars can't handle, and if I know Quita like I think I know her then I know that most likely she was broke by now.

"Twenty thousand."

"What?"

"You heard me. Twenty thousand dollars! That's how much I'll give you. That's more than enough for you to get yourself a place and everything you need for the baby before it's born. Give me some time to get some things in order, and once you give birth, we can come to some arrangement about custody and visitation, but I don't want to hear a word of this shit from anyone. Do you understand? If anyone asks who that kid's father is, don't mention my name. It ain't nobody's business anyway, and the last thing I need is for my girl to find out about this before I have the opportunity to break the news to her on my terms."

The line was silent for a while Quita pondered on my proposal.

"Okay. I guess that's fair. I guess my only question is...when do I get paid?"

36

Royale'

My hair, makeup, and lashes were all done, and the Gucci dress that I bought to go with my new purse hugged every curve on my body. I examined myself in the full-length mirror and was pleased with what I saw. I'm sure my man would be too. He promised to make tonight one that I wouldn't forget, so I was more than excited to see just what he had in store. That man is always doing something.

After many hours of getting ready, I finally emerged down the winding stairs of our home. Kaseeno stood at the bottom of the staircase, staring up at me with all love and admiration in his eyes. I took my precious time stepping down each stair careful not to trip or stumble in my Gucci leather platform boots. Just like the gentleman I've always known him to be, Kaseeno extended his hand, and I grabbed ahold to it as I made my way down the last steps. He looked dapper and matched my fly in his three-piece suit and Gucci bow tie.

"You look exquisite, my lady."

"You're very dapper as well, my fellow," I replied as we

headed out to our awaiting carriage, his 2020 black-on-black Range Rover.

We rode down the highway for about twenty minutes before we arrived at a strip mall in Sumerlin. I was confused because this didn't look like the typical fancy restaurant or romantic setting that I had become accustomed to on our date nights. Still, by now, I know not to question Kaseeno and his lavish surprises, so I just climbed out of the car and latched on to his arm as we walked to the door.

I figured this must be one of the many locations he owns since he pulled a key from his pocket and opened the door. He flicked the lights, and I buried my face into my hands at the sight of all of our friends and family.

"SUPRISE!!!"

The décor in the spa was beautifully decorated with white and teal colors. Everything was coordinated from the floor tiles down to the salon chairs and wall art. There were shelves filled with nail polish from the front door all the way to the back. I was in awe. This was the surprise that tops all surprises, and I have no idea when and how he had the time to pull it off.

"How did you..." I turned around to find Kaseeno on bended knee, holding open a velvet box. Inside was the most beautiful and flawless ring that I had ever seen. I covered my mouth, gasping for air. While no one else around us seemed shocked, this proposal had really caught me off guard. He took my hand, and I could feel the sweat from his palms.

"Royale' Lee, baby girl, there are no words that can express just how beautifully amazing you truly are. Since the moment that I laid eyes on you, I knew that you were someone that I had to know, and since I've had the pleasure of knowing you, I'm absolutely sure that I don't want to spend another moment without you. It hasn't been one hundred percent easy, but you've remained by my side, where I want you to be for the rest of our lives. I guess what I'm trying to say... I mean, I know what I'm trying to ask is... Will you marry me?"

The tears that had threatened to fall were now rolling down my cheeks. I felt my lips part, but before I could say yes, the sound of shattering glass damn near busted my eardrum. I saw Quita's truck speed off into the darkness. She had thrown a brick with an ultrasound attached to it right through the window of my new spa.

TO BE CONTINUED...

About the Author

K. Brijon, began her writing career in 2006 as a Screenwriter. Her first writing credit was for a short film entitled Reflections which aired on BET Networks in 2007. Born and raised in the Chicago land area, K. received her Bachelors of Arts from Columbia College Chicago in 2011. K. Brijon signed to Mz. Lady P Presents in October of 2017 and released her first published novel Cadillac & Journee a Twisted Hood Affair in February 2018. For K. writing is a way to both express herself and also take readers to new heights. To learn more about this author please follow her Reading Group on Facebook entitled K's Reading Korner.

Made in the USA
Columbia, SC
10 November 2020